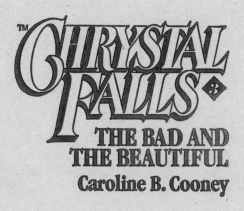

CHRYSTAL FALLS 3

THE BAD AND THE BEAUTIFUL

Caroline B. Cooney

SCHOLASTIC INC.
New York Toronto London Auckland Sydney

ISBN 0-590-33690-8

12 11 10 9 8 7 6 5 4 3 2 1   11   5 6 7 8 9/8 0/9

Printed in the U.S.A.   06

THE BAD AND THE BEAUTIFUL

CHRYSTAL FALLS

The Wrong Side of Love
Breaking the Rules
The Bad and the Beautiful
The Morning After
A Loss of Innocence
Forbidden Love

Chapter
One

"Mother and I are going to New York to get my dress, of course," said Chelsea, laughing. She tossed her head. Her short yellow hair flipped over her eyes.

It was the "of course" that infuriated Karen Pickett. Nobody in Chrystal Falls went to New York for a dress *of course*.

"When the mall actually opens," Dawn Newhouse said, "none of us will have to go out of town for anything! I can just hardly wait. Sixty-eight stores. Lord & Taylor's, Bloomingdale's, The Country Shoppe, The Bridal Wreath —"

The listening crowd of high school girls hooted with laughter. "Dawn Newhouse," they teased. "Are you planning marriage already? We knew you were getting pretty fond of Pete, but still. . . ."

Dawn blushed. She was more than fond of Pete. She adored him. But his moody temperament had not changed. She was so unsure of him. It was exciting to daydream about a future with Pete Carter, but not so easy to establish anything with him in the present. One month he would see her; the next he was aloof.

"Tell us about the new mall," begged one of the girls.

Chelsea Chrystal perched on top of the lunch table, like a princess with her subjects gathered round. She was glowing with excitement. After months and months of construction, the mall was finally nearing completion. Every city in America had a decent shopping mall except her own city, and now, finally, Chrystal Falls would have one, too.

Chrystal Mall.

And who would cut the scarlet ribbon? Who would dance the first dance at the great opening gala?

She, Chelsea Chrystal, heiress to the Chrystal Mill fortune.

"The center of the mall will rise three stories," said Chelsea, spacing the floors with her graceful hands. "It has a glass roof, like a castle. There are huge prisms and chandeliers of crystal to catch the sun and reflect tiny rainbows all over the walls. Glass elevators carry shoppers from floor to floor. The balconies are lined with plant boxes, and ivy and pink geraniums will cascade down. In the very center of the mall there is a crystal fountain, with stars under the water, and lights to make it glitter."

Chelsea's enthusiasm was infectious. All the girls wanted a mall to shop at, and never had they heard of any shopping mall as beautiful as this one would be. Theirs was a dreary mill town, and painfully divided between the rich kids and the mill hands' kids — but they would *all* share the mall.

"The governor and both senators will be there," said Chelsea, and the girls were as impressed as she knew they would be. Chelsea thought to herself, I'll dance with them. I'll be the belle of this ball.

Karen Pickett left the knot of excited girls, trying to contain her anger. *Of course* Chelsea was going to New York City to get a dress. Honestly! Who did Chelsea think she was?

Princess, thought Karen bitterly.

It was true that Chelsea was beautiful and elegant and wealthy — but did she have to throw it in their faces all the time? Karen would be lucky if she didn't have to wear the same dress she had worn to all the sophomore and two of the junior class dances. And here was Chelsea Chrystal, *of course*, getting her dress in New York.

And what do I get? thought Karen. I get to launder my waitress uniform so I can wait table on Chelsea at the country club.

Karen saw her boyfriend Mitch and ran to catch up to him. Mitch irritated her at times, with his easy acceptance of his position in life, but he was comforting to be with.

"Every time I think I've come to terms with Chelsea and all her money and her family's snobbish treatment of the rest of us, something happens and all my bad feelings surface," Karen said to Mitch. They linked arms and he kissed her soft hair. "You know what?" said Karen.

"What?" said Mitch.

"She's going to New York to get her dress. *Of course.*"

Mitch just laughed. "Big deal. You'll still be the prettiest girl there. It doesn't matter what you wear."

"A lot you know, Mitch. It matters. All this is just going to reinforce Chels' view of herself as Princess of the Land."

"Relax," was Mitch's advice. "And along with relaxing, quit your job at the country club. The mill layoff is over, your father's back at work, you don't need the money so desperately. Why torture yourself with that job? When exams are over you can look for a job that doesn't rub your nerves raw."

Karen nodded. Mitch was right. She would give the club two weeks' notice this afternoon. "On the other hand, if I keep working, I can afford a nice dress, too," she said to Mitch.

Mitch didn't want to hear about dresses.

4

The gala Chrystal Mall dance was for anybody who could spring for the price of the tickets, and Mitch was looking forward to it, and he truly didn't care what Karen wore. Karen would be the best dancer there anyhow. Chelsea Chrystal could take all the expensive dancing lessons she wanted, but his Karen would outshine her anyhow; her athletic grace and her small, compact frame made her a joy to dance with.

Besides, the money raised at the dance was going to go to help Halfway House. Mitch liked the whole idea of that place. A home for a kid to go to when he was having troubles. Not a detention center — not a place with bars — but a home away from home, when a kid just couldn't make it otherwise. How many times had Mitch felt like that? And maybe his own brothers, who did end up in prison, would have fared better if they'd had a Halfway House to go to when the pressure was on.

"If she just hadn't said *of course* she's going to New York," Karen went on.

Mitch shook his head. "I can tell this is going to be the topic of conversation for weeks to come. Did Chelsea go to New York? Does the dress look as if it required a trip to New York? Is it fair to the mill workers of Chrystal Falls that — "

Karen stopped him with a kiss. She planted it very firmly on his still moving lips, and he stopped talking, grinned briefly even though she was kissing him, and then kissed her back.

"Don't smile when I kiss you," she said severely. "It's very difficult to kiss a spreading mouth."

The bell rang loudly, and they separated for the last class of the day.

Behind them walked another couple.

Dawn and Pete had hair the same color: glossy black. Pete's was thick and unruly; Dawn's clung to her head and shoulders. Their bodies were very close and as Dawn turned her face toward Pete's, they seemed to be a mass of dark hair, meeting.

On and off since Dawn had moved to Chrystal Falls she and Pete had been drawn together. They had not dated much. They had tended to meet, instead, while Dawn walked the dog, or Pete headed for work, or they'd secretly gone for a pizza or a Coke. Dawn loved their meetings and their talk — and their infrequent kisses and embraces — but the relationship mystified her. In all the months she had lived in this mill town she had not figured out why they all *cared* so much. Who lived where, who worked where, who was Hill, who was Mill — I mean, thought Dawn disgustedly, who needs it? Life is tough enough without all that snobbery and separation.

Dawn wanted to be with Pete just the way they were now. Arms wrapped around each other, thoughts entangled with each other.

6

But she knew by now how it would go.

Pete, who judged her by her friends, would vanish as quickly as he had come, and all the emotions he had stirred up in her would be left. Dawn Newhouse liked everybody. Their street addresses and their parents' occupations bored her.

But Pete, whose father was a union organizer and whose history was a little rough, was not the sort of boy the country club set thought Dawn should be seen with. And Dawn, because her mother and uncle were doctors in the town, was definitely in the country club set.

She looked up at him — at that dark face with the jaw set in a belligerent way, and the eyes like the lull before the storm. She smiled at him, yearning to have him ask her out for a real date: a date in public. She wanted them to be known in the school as a couple; she wanted people to smile when they saw the pair; she wanted people to think of her as part of Pete, and Pete as part of her.

But whether Pete would allow such a thing, Dawn did not know. Pete Carter kept his feelings and his thoughts well hidden. He was hiding them now.

He listened to Dawn talk about the Chrystal Mall and chose not to tell her the history of that mall.

It had not been Chrystal land, originally, that large flat stretch at the bend in Rapid

River. There had been warehouses there. One of the warehouses burned to the ground, and the owner sold out cheap, and pretty soon it was Chrystal land, and soon after that, it was announced that there would be a Chrystal Mall built upon it.

The origins of the fire were uncertain. But only in the eyes of the police.

Pete was sure *he* knew who had set the fire. But why tell Dawn? Dawn was a realist who had been through a lot in the last year — her father's early death, a traumatic move across the country — but Dawn was given to thinking the best of people. It was a trait Pete did not share.

Dawn thought highly of the Chrystal clan. But in Pete's opinion, Chelsea, self-appointed princess of the high school, had a brother who was dirt.

Some people were just plain good, like Dawn. Some were losers, like that stupid girl friend of Chelsea's, Perky. But some, like Montgomery Chrystal, were scum.

Dawn was talking about the mall. For reasons Pete couldn't figure out she was most interested in the shoe stores. Pete wanted to take Dawn to that dance at Chrystal Mall with a fierceness that surprised him. He was not interested in dances, totally not interested in the social gatherings of the country club set — and yet he was as eager for this ball as any of the girls. He did not know what to make of himself. He thought constantly of the dance: of getting Dawn flowers, and renting a tuxedo, and dancing under the glittering sparkle of the finest mall in the state.

Neither of them had a class to go to, so they went to the student lounge instead, and sat on the stone floor by one of the huge windows that looked down over the mill town toward Rapid River. A weak winter sun tried to warm the stone floor but still they had to sit on their folded coats to keep comfortable.

"Do you think I'm selfish?" said Dawn.

He stared at her small, neat features and burst out laughing. "You? Selfish?"

"Yes, me, selfish."

"What on earth made you think that?"

Dawn frowned and he saw that she was serious. "My mother is out there saving lives," she said. "Every day, all day, she's in that emergency room taking care of people. And what am I doing? Mooching."

"You're still in high school," said Pete. "What else can you do? You can't save the world until you have your high school diploma, at least."

She made a face at him. "Don't tease. This is important. I know I can't save the world, now or ever. The world is beyond me. But I feel like saving *somebody*."

"Save me," suggested Pete. "Save me from

9

sexual desire that is going to wipe me off the map if we don't go to a motel somewhere and — "

Dawn brushed her hand at him, but giggled, pleased in spite of herself. He caught her fluttering hand and traced patterns on her palm with his rough workman's hands. Dawn struggled to remember what she had been saying, but it wasn't easy, aware only of his touch.

A week ago, her mother had staggered out of bed at two in the morning and made a dash for the hospital, where a patient had combined hard drugs with a fast-moving car and a bridge abutment. Dr. Newhouse had saved the young man. Not that he wouldn't drive like a maniac as soon as he was up and about — but Barbara Newhouse had given back a life, and the life had a second chance.

It seemed to Dawn that never in her whole life had she done anything charitable. She'd hardly even given a dollar, let alone a life. What was she but a useless appendage to society?

"You complain about the Chrystals," said Dawn, "but the truth is that that family has done wonderful things for this town."

"They're bloodsuckers," said Pete and he dropped her hand.

They both stared at their hands, and wished they hadn't gotten onto this topic, and yet they couldn't drop it.

10

"Grandmother Chrystal," Dawn pointed out, "started the museum forty-five years ago. And the visiting symphony. And it's Chelsea's mother who runs the historical society that preserved the first house ever built in Chrystal Falls. And the Chrystals gave and maintain the Rose Gardens near the Town Hall. And they're the ones raising the money to keep Halfway House open."

Pete controlled a sneer. The only reason the Chrystals wanted Halfway House open was that any minute now Monty Chrystal would get kicked out of his latest expensive boarding school and be shipped home in disgrace, and they wanted a place to stow him other than their own mansion. Who would want to live with dirt like Monty Chrystal? Certainly not the Chrystals themselves. They had their image to keep up, after all.

This was a family whose fleet of Mercedes all had special license plates: CRSTL 1, CRSTL 2 — on up to Princess Chelsea, whose white convertible was CRSTL 3.

Ought to have a nice little number done up for Monty, thought Pete Carter grimly. ARSON 1.

But he said nothing to Dawn.

She would accuse him of judging people too harshly. She would say it wasn't Monty's fault he was born a rich Chrystal, and that Pete was wrong for judging Monty on the basis of his inherited bankbook. In Pete's opinion Dawn didn't judge people enough, and someday it was going to be the undoing of her.

They sat silently, uncomfortably, trying to keep from arguing. They wanted to be peacefully in love, not fighting, but this was easier to dream about than to achieve.

In Maine, along the northern coast, up a twisting, rock-strewn river, it was still the dead of winter. Ice crackled and snow glistened. The night was cloudy and the wind was fierce.

Nobody saw the tall, husky shape that crept through the heavy shrubbery of the prep school campus toward the big old Colonial house that had once housed a sea captain's family of eleven children, and was now divided into faculty apartments.

Nobody heard thick boots crunching through old snow.

Nobody saw the tall, husky shape crouch down and pour liquid over dry, rustling leaves and twigs that the winter wind had tossed up by the back steps of the history teacher's entryway.

Nobody heard the rasp of a match against a tiny box, nor saw the flicker of the match as it drew near the tinder.

But the flames.

They saw the flames.

Scarlet and gold, like tongues of eagerness,

the flames licked the dry old wood, reaching for the sleeping history professor. The fire crackled with laughter and burned with joy.

Or was it the tall, husky shape that laughed and burned with joy?

Dr. Barbara Newhouse flopped backwards on the huge couch. One of her shoes fell off and the other didn't. Her son, Josh, Dawn's older brother, tugged gently at his mother's other shoe, and when both her feet were free, she wiggled her toes gladly and said, "You know what's going to kill me? Not malaria, not smallpox, not hepatitis. Fallen arches."

Her two children grinned. Josh, getting to the important things immediately, said, "What's for supper?"

"I love it," said his mother to the wall. "I put in a ten-hour day, collapse on the couch with terminal feet, and the kid wants to know what we're having for supper."

"I was addressing my sister," said Josh with dignity. "Dawn is responsible for supper tonight because I did it last night."

"You call yesterday's meal supper?" said Dawn indignantly. "That was a cardboard box shoved in the microwave."

"There was food in the box," Josh pointed out.

"How you love to exaggerate," said Dawn. "Anyway, for supper we are having lasagna.

Dawn's own. Well, actually, Pete's mother's own. I was over at Pete's this afternoon and his mother gave me the recipe."

"You and Pete are getting pretty tight," observed Josh.

Dawn shrugged. If only that were true! It was the first time she'd been in Pete Carter's house. She had talked more to Mrs. Carter than to Pete. She had never known anybody as prickly as Pete Carter. But then, he reflected the whole town: Chrystal Falls was as prickly as a porcupine on everything.

Chrystal Falls made her think of Chrystal Mall, which brought her to a central issue. "When are we going to get our dresses for the dance, Mother?" she said. "It isn't that far off. We have to start looking now."

"You really want to go?" said her mother dismally. "I thought I'd just lie around and hope nobody ends up in the emergency room."

"Of course we want to go!" cried Dawn. "This is the social event of the year! And you have to go, too, Mom. It's time you started to have a social life of your own."

Nobody responded to this. She had brought up a taboo subject. Never once had Josh and Dawn spoken of the fact that their mother, who was still young and very lovely, would probably remarry one day. Josh dated. Dawn dated. But the idea of their mother dating was scary.

The three Newhouses looked away from each other, the light bantering over, the nervous reality of life back. Dawn felt tears burning her eyes, as she remembered the father who should have made the fourth member of the family.

When she spoke, her voice sounded strange. Her throat had thickened and she had to turn away from her mother to hide her shining eyes. "I'll set the table," said Dawn. "Does everyone want ice water?"

"Pepsi," said Josh.

Dawn arranged the silver on the delicately flowered placemats, wedging herself back and forth in the effort of setting it.

"You know, we really must move," said her mother, watching. "This apartment is miniscule. We can't even walk around the table. We have to squeeze around it."

"Where would we go?" said Dawn. She wasn't sure she liked the idea of a move. Now that she had been meeting Pete so frequently after supper — as she walked the dog and Pete walked her — another location was a threat.

"I wanted the least possible amount of space to take care of when we got here," said her mother, "because I was so nervous about being on my own. And it had to be an apartment so that a superintendent would be in charge of any real problems. And it had to be within walking distance of the hospital. But I don't think any of those reasons matter now. Perhaps we should start house-hunting."

Josh groaned. "Let's not and say we did."

"You like it in this cramped box?" asked their mother.

He shrugged. He was getting very tall, and the shrug seemed to threaten the ceiling. "We've had enough change in our lives," he said. "Dad dying. A big move. New school, new friends." He made a terrible, exaggerated face. "New relatives."

The relative who made him shudder could only be Aunt Vicki. A dreadful woman. Nobody could imagine how Uncle Walter, who was beloved by everybody in Chrystal Falls, could have married her, and even less could they imagine how their son Tim could have turned out so wonderfully, even though he had lived with her for nineteen years.

"Unless we move in next door to Vicki on Canturbury Lane," said Dawn, "she'll say we're going to a slum and it reflects poorly on her."

Dr. Newhouse tucked herself into a little ball. Josh tossed the afghan over her and she snuggled under it. "I don't think we need to take Aunt Vicki's opinions into consideration," she said. "But it's still winter and I can't think about house hunting when I'm still thinking about ice. Maybe this summer, though. When flowers are in bloom and spirits are high."

16

"Not to mention prices," said Josh, and they all laughed.

Dawn took the lasagna out of the oven and sniffed the wonderful spices of Mrs. Carter's tomato sauce recipe, and she found herself worrying about all the families who wouldn't have something good to eat that night.

And what am I doing about it? thought Dawn. Nothing. I must think of something to do that is *good*.

Oddly enough, Chelsea Chrystal was having the exact same thought.

"Daddy?" she said to her gray-haired, elegant, lawyer father. "How much will we raise from the ball?"

"Quite a bit," said her father, without giving details. He had never been impressed with his older daughter's ability to pay attention to numbers.

"I've never been to Halfway House," Chelsea said. "Is it a nice place? What will they do with the money? Build something? Or pay staff? Or what?"

Mr. Chrystal had never been there either. But to their surprise, Elizabeth Chrystal had a ready answer. "It's next to the country club," said Chelsea's mother. "Near the ninth hole where the course takes that big loop. Where we're always losing balls in the hemlocks."

They nodded. They all played a good deal

17

of golf, although tennis was the family sport. "Beyond the evergreens in the old Victorian house with seven bedrooms. We renovated it four or five years ago with the money we raised from the sale of Impressionist paintings. It has resident parents and they take care of six or seven young boys at a time."

"How young is young?" questioned Amy Chrystal. Amy was thirteen. Her life revolved around facts. She had kept the *Guinness Book of World Records* by her bed since second grade, and her favorite books were almanacs, encyclopedias, and financial sheets. She and her grandfather, Judge Chrystal, sat together every evening studying the stock market.

Amy's father never looked at Amy without wishing that his son Monty had Amy's personality. Not that he didn't adore Amy, with her boundless energy and her bubbly personality and her grasp of facts — but oh, to have a son like that, instead of a son like. . . .

Well. No point in dwelling on that. Monty was safely off in Maine and with any luck they'd bring him around. He'd get an education and maybe even pick up good manners to boot.

"Ages thirteen to nineteen," said Mrs. Chrystal. "By and large they're nice boys. The child I work with has abusive parents, both alcoholics, very rough on him. But the child hasn't done anything wrong. He just needs love."

None of them had even known that Mrs. Chrystal was working with a boy at Halfway House. It was typical of her. She was very self-contained about her work. She had a fragile presence, as if one good puff and she would blow away, and yet she controlled a network of charity and social enterprises that literally required a staff. It was beyond Alexander Chrystal how he and his beautiful wife had ever spawned a son like Monty. With all Elizabeth's love, to end up with a son who —

He cut off the thought. After all these years he could not bring himself to admit the truth of Montgomery Chrystal.

Chelsea said, "When do you think we can go to New York for my dress, Mother?"

Her mother reflected. "The next two weekends are impossible. I have too many commitments. Perhaps after that. But when do your exams fall, dear?"

"She doesn't know," said Amy. "She never knows. Do you think Chels has ever studied in her whole entire life?"

"Brilliant people don't have to study," said Chelsea. "They just *absorb*."

"If your grades in French are any example," said Amy, "the old Chrystal blotter paper is getting a little dry."

"Oh, be quiet!" said Chelsea, who had never intended to tell her parents about that last French test. "Mother, may I be excused?"

Her mother smiled. "If you're going to ap-

19

ply yourself to your French, you certainly may."

Amy opened her mouth to make a wise remark but stopped when she caught Chelsea's glare. They didn't fight much and almost never when their grandparents were at the table. They smirked at each other instead. Chelsea circled the table, kissing her mother, grandmother, father, and grandfather on the forehead, and went to her room, where she didn't even open her French book. Instead she telephoned Dawn, who she always liked talking to.

They talked mostly about dresses and the ball, which was still weeks off. And then Chelsea said, "My mother volunteers at Halfway House. I didn't even know about it. She works with a little abused kid who needs love. Isn't that sweet?"

Dawn was startled by the insensitivity of Chelsea's comment, but she knew Chelsea couldn't help responding that way.

"It's wonderful!" exclaimed Dawn. She especially liked the part about nobody knowing Mrs. Chrystal was doing this. She does good deeds without bragging about them, thought Dawn. I'll have to tell Pete. Maybe he can revise his opinion of her when he hears that. Or maybe it will just start another argument between us.

Dawn considered talking to Chelsea about Pete but decided against it. Chelsea would be

20

the first to admit that Pete was handsome and built and sexy — but she would not consider that that meant anything. "He's a mill hand's kid," Chelsea would say, irritated. "You have to aim higher than that, Dawn. You're too good for somebody who's going to drink beer and tighten bolts for a lifetime."

Dawn thought, Perhaps *I* could volunteer at Halfway House, too! *That* would be a good deed. A start on saving the world.

She laughed at herself, but still, she liked the idea.

Far away, in Maine, lethal smoke crept under a door and slid unseen toward a sleeping victim.

Chapter
Two

"Chelsea Chrystal," said the metallic-voiced loudspeaker, "report to the principal's office please. Chelsea Chrystal."

She was in English when they called, and the class was being silly because they had a substitute. "You're in trouble now," said Ryan Simpson, grinning. "Life in the fast lane finally caught up to you, Chels."

"It's all that criminal activity," teased one of the girls.

Chelsea laughed. She loved any kind of attention — what normal person doesn't? — and the good-natured teasing of the class pleased her.

"It's probably your mother," said Dawn. "She just can't wait to fly to New York for that dress, and she's chartered a jet to take you there this moment."

22

"That must be it," agreed Chelsea, tossing her hair. "The boutiques in New York probably heard I was coming and *begged* me to hurry."

"Now, class," said the substitute fussily. "Come to order."

Nobody paid the slightest bit of attention to the teacher.

Chelsea drew out her moment, gathering her books slowly, stacking them, jangling the bracelets on her wrist, and flirting with Josh and Ryan both, who were sitting in the back row. This irked Ryan and amused Josh.

There were few things Chelsea Chrystal enjoyed more than center stage. She was often amazed at girls who shrank from attention. Some girls always wore clothing in beige and pastels, so that nobody noticed them; or didn't bother with their hair even when it could be lovely; or never spoke up even when they had a funny observation to make.

That was incomprehensible to Chelsea.

Life should be a party, and just because it was English class was no reason to stop partying. "Off to my prison sentence," she said lightly to the class.

Two of the boys offered to share her cell.

The teacher scolded them and Chelsea said, "Highest bidder gets to bunk with me."

"Miss Chrystal!" exclaimed the substitute, not at all amused, and Chelsea laughed and left the room.

It was a very sunny day, and the brightness poured through the windows and shone on Chelsea like a spotlight. She sauntered down the halls, enjoying the memory of the silly teasing in English class and wondering vaguely what the principal might want. She had never done anything wrong, so she had no guilty conscience to trouble her. It was probably her mother changing a dental appointment, or something boring like that.

She greeted the secretaries in the office rather gaily, and they greeted her by name. There were hundreds of kids at Chrystal Falls High — but Chelsea was known by everyone from the janitors to the substitutes. The principal called out to her, "Just a phone call, Chelsea. Take it in my office."

She walked languidly into his office, setting her books down on his desk, claiming it as her own territory. Freeing herself from the strap of her dangling purse, she picked up the phone and said hello.

It was her father on the line.

She knew immediately there was something terribly wrong. Alexander Chrystal had never telephoned her at school; that was her mother's field. She stood very still, thinking — *death*? *accident*? Even before she answered him, she was afraid. "Hello, Daddy, what's wrong?"

"Come home, Chelsea," he said. "Immediately."

Her hands became covered with cold sweat, so that the phone slipped in her grasp. "What is it?" she said. The principal was watching, listening. She struggled to stay expressionless. She thought — somebody is hurt. Is it Grand Lily? Did she have a heart attack? Is it mother? Did she have a car accident?

Her throat hurt and her heart raced.

"Just come home," was the terse answer. Her father spent his life in court in stressful situations; stress was nothing new to him; and yet his voice sounded at the breaking point.

"Is somebody hurt?" she managed to say.

"Nobody is hurt. It's Monty."

She wanted to smash the telephone on the principal's desk. Monty. Oh, how could he? How could she be related to this rotten person who was always in some terrible trouble? How could this be happening when her life was so perfect, so filled with sunshine?

She knew Monty well. Too well. She knew just how bad it could be. And if her father was making the call, it meant her mother was too upset to touch the telephone. And that meant the worst possible news. It meant they wanted her home before the news became public.

Public.

She hung up very carefully, thanking the principal for letting her use the phone, and just as carefully she stacked her books again and sauntered out of the office. She did not tell anyone she was going home. Better to cut

25

class than to explain family troubles. She was a Chrystal. She would *never* discuss her family with secretaries and clerks, and in Chelsea's opinion the principal was simply a clerk who ran the school.

Public.

She loved center stage, she loved attention — but not this kind. Not the scandal and the horror that followed Monty wherever he went.

In the hall she could hear the faint, comforting buzz of schoolwork in all its variations. She felt horribly distant from it. Some terrible thing had happened in her life, and she knew none of the details, but from experience she knew one thing.

It was going to be horrible.

Outside it was very cold, and the yellow light of the sun was merely a coating on the ice. She shivered and willed herself not to cry. Chrystals did not cry. Not in public, anyhow.

Monty. Monty, who had hurt their pets and abused their ponies. Monty, who set aside his grandmother's heart medicine and slid aspirin in its place.

Nobody but the family knew about that, and not all the family. Amy had never been told. She was considered the child of the family, and it was understood that she was to be protected.

And then there were the scandals the whole town knew about.

Last summer Monty had caddied at the

country club. Was it mere coincidence that the houses of the men and women for whom Monty caddied were vandalized when the families were away on vacation? Monty knew who would be in Europe on business, who was visiting cousins in California, who was fishing in Maine.

The police questioned him, but there was no proof. Monty was free to insult the police, and he certainly did. If it had not been for Perky Palmer's father — her father's law partner — whose criminal experience was very useful for Monty, Chelsea had a feeling he would have stayed in jail just for the way he talked back to the police.

It helped, if you were going to be criminal, to be very smart. Monty had one inheritance from the Chrystals — brains. Nobody had ever been able to pin anything on him. He was too crafty.

Chelsea got to her white convertible, with its magnificent red leather interior. It gave her no pleasure. It was testimony to the real truth. No amount of money could buy family happiness.

At least, she thought grimly, starting the engine, I can drive to our doom in style.

From English class, high on the third floor, Karen Pickett watched Chelsea's progress across the parking lot to her car. Of course Chelsea walked across the grass in the circle.

Forbidden. It had just been reseeded in the vain hope that no student would drive over the circle and leave ruts in the grass. But Chelsea had no use for rules. She took the straightest path to her car and it was just too bad that there was forbidden territory between her and it. Anybody else, thought Karen, would get caught. Nobody sees Chelsea do anything but good things.

In the seat in front of her, Ryan Simpson also gazed out the window at Chelsea's slim, wind-blown figure. Karen had no use for Ryan. His last name fit him. He was a simp. He lacked courage and honor. The very first week they were in town, Dawn's brother Josh whipped Ryan in tennis. Ryan was such a poor sportsman he hardly shook hands with the victor afterwards. Karen detested weak people like that.

But Chelsea dated him.

Probably, in Karen's opinion, because Ryan worshipped her. Ryan was like a puppy wagging its tail around Chelsea. He might as well be wearing a leash and collar. It would be interesting to see Chels date a *real* boy: somebody with a real personality, who would argue with her and say no to her. It would be like watching television, seeing which person won. Karen would put her money on Chelsea. Nothing mattered more to Chelsea than winning.

Karen forgot that nothing mattered more to

28

her, either. One reason she and Chelsea did
not get along — could not get along — was
that they were both so strong and sure. There
was not room for two of them in the same
gathering, not when they were of such different backgrounds.

People said that Chelsea's father and grandfather had bought Monty's freedom twice last
year. Once when the buildings were burned
on the land where Chrystal Mall was now
going up, and once when all those rich types at
the club got robbed and Monty was the like-
liest suspect.

Karen didn't think the men would stoop to
that. From all her parents said, Mr. Chrystal
was a sound lawyer and Judge Chrystal an
ethical judge. But at the same time they
were tricky, they were shrewd, and maybe
they were without ethics. How could you suc-
ceed in a ruthless business like running a mill
if you weren't?

Far below, Chelsea swung her car out of
the parking lot. Because it was easier, Chelsea
drove out the in.

Karen shook her head. Of course there
wasn't a policeman around; there would never
be one when Chelsea was breaking the rules.

She just wished there would be one someday when Monty Chrystal broke the rules. For
a while Karen's own brother Johnnie had
been very close friends with Monty. She had
lived in fear that those two would be friends

29

right up to their life sentences in prison. But Johnnie, thank goodness, had straightened out. More or less. Monty Chrystal had gotten even more bent. The boys rarely saw each other now, because Monty was rarely in town.

There was one thing the Chrystal fortunes could not buy.

A decent character for their only son.

The driveway to the family home was long and impressive, lined with beautifully kept shrubbery, mostly evergreens that stayed lovely all year. The holly hedge had been planted two generations ago, and now it gleamed a Christmas green and sparkled with scarlet berries.

The fine iron gates, so rarely closed, were a quiet announcement that beyond the gates and the holly stood a house of importance.

Usually Chelsea loved turning into her drive. You couldn't see the house at all from the road, and there was always a faint sense of mystery. She loved the instant when the mansion appeared before her eyes, and she knew that it was *hers* and always would be.

Today Chelsea felt nothing but fear. Crawling, sickening fear. What had Monty done now?

Parked in the circle in front of the house was Mr. Palmer's car. So they had already called in the criminal lawyer. Swallowing her nausea, Chelsea parked behind him and went to her door. She did not have to open it. Her mother was standing behind it, waiting for her.

Whatever it was, it was very bad. Chelsea could tell from the frozen, shrinking way her mother stood. Elizabeth Chrystal could organize anything with grace and efficiency. But when it came to handling emotional troubles, she simply vanished.

Chelsea hugged her mother, but there was no response. Already Elizabeth Chrystal was turning into herself, hiding. "Are they in the study?" said Chelsea. "Let's join them." Get it over with, she thought. Knowing the truth is better than shivering with apprehension.

She wished they had called Amy, too. Amy was thirteen, scarcely a child; in any event, Amy was the most realistic of them all and could probably handle it better than the people trying to protect her.

Protect me, too, thought Chelsea, and she struggled not to cry. She walked on thick, lush carpet beneath the oil portraits of her illustrious ancestors. *Protect me, too, please?*

She drew her mother into the study. Mr. Palmer ushered Mrs. Chrystal into the leather wing chair, taking the fine, carved wooden chair for himself. Chelsea perched on the vast wooden chest her father had bought in Holland years ago.

There was a moment of silence. Chelsea prepared herself. Her father said without looking directly at his family, "Monty is coming home. His plane will land this afternoon. He was caught setting fire to the residence of a faculty member who flunked him."

Chelsea was unable to repress a shudder. Her joints hurt as if she was old and had arthritis. She said in a thin, terrified voice, "Was anybody hurt?"

"No," said her father. His tight voice told them all that he, Alexander Chrystal, had been hurt. Hurt terribly. Once again his son, his oldest child, had shown bad blood.

"Somebody in the building was up that night, calming a crying infant. They saw the flames before they really caught hold. There was a lot of smoke but not much damage. The teacher didn't even go to the emergency room."

"Why is Monty coming home?" demanded Chelsea. "Why isn't he going to jail?"

"He is not being charged with anything," said Mr. Palmer.

"Not being charged?" cried Chelsea. *"Why not?"*

"What's the matter with you?" said her father furiously. "Do you *want* your brother in jail?"

"I want him to pay for what he does," said Chelsea. "It's wrong to let him weasel out of every single terrible thing he does. He'll never learn! He'll go right on doing awful things, and you'll be helping him!"

The men looked uncomfortable.

Chelsea glared at them. "Why does he always get off?" she cried out.

Her father said heavily, "The school is having a lot of trouble with the local community, Chelsea. They don't want any more bad publicity. If word gets out that students are torching houses, they might have to shut down. They'd rather just send him back to us."

Again. He had gotten away with something criminal *again*.

He would come home laughing at the stupid world. He would sneer at her, and at all her friends. But they would be afraid to sneer back at Monty. It was Chelsea herself who would bear the brunt of the gossip, and the fear of what Monty would do next, and the shame of whatever he had done in the past.

She thought, Josh and Dawn probably don't know anything about my brother. They haven't lived here long enough to pick up all the gossip. But now the talk will start up again, and they'll hear everything.

Chelsea could have wept. Bad enough that Dawn, who was becoming a good friend, would hear about her terrible brother. But for Josh to know was truly hideous. She wanted Josh to love her. She wanted Josh to yearn for her and ache for her and think of her every moment he was awake, and maybe in his sleep, too.

He was interested. That was all, so far. She didn't want mere interest. She wanted passionate interest.

Oh, wait till he meets Montgomery Chrystal, thought Chelsea, sick to her stomach. He won't want any part of me then.

But Chelsea Chrystal did not cry. She was made of sterner stuff, and she intended to cope with Josh and handle Monty and come out a winner. It was her mother who broke down.

They were all stunned. Her father and Mr. Palmer stared in shock when Elizabeth Chrystal bent over, a desperate, rasping moan coming from her soul. Her small fists bunched, the beautiful long nails shining, Chelsea's mother pounded on Alexander Chrystal's desk and screamed at the top of her lungs. *"I cannot bear it!"*

Chelsea quivered. She could not imagine her elegant, reserved mother having a temper tantrum.

"Do you understand, Alexander?" screamed Mrs. Chrystal. "I. Can. Not. Bear. It."

Her words were separated by gasps and slamming fists.

George Palmer said, as if inquiring of a hostile witness on the stand, "Can't bear what, Elizabeth?"

She whirled on him. "I cannot bear to have that boy back in this house. I *will not* have him back here. I *can not* live with him!"

Mr. Chrystal said, "Now, dear."

Mr. Palmer said, "Now, Elizabeth, really."

Chelsea thought, *Men*. She put her arms around her mother and said, "Mother, stop crying. There's a simple solution. Somebody will meet Monty at the airport and take him somewhere else, that's all."

"It's not that easy," her father argued. "Monty has a pretty checkered past. Schools don't like to take him on. And when they telephone this school in Maine, and find out why he was expelled so abruptly ... well. ..."

How fragile her mother was! She had never clasped her mother like this. Chelsea was painfully aware that her mother might really not be able to bear it, if Monty returned. What would happen? she thought. Would Mother leave us? Would she have a breakdown? Would *she* be the one who ended up in an institution, when it's Monty who deserves it?

Chelsea refused to be beaten, or to allow her mother to be beaten. She was furious with the two lawyers for standing there like helpless little boys, hoping it would all go away. She said, "Well, call the Judge." Her grandfather was the Judge even to his grandchildren. "He'll be able to think of something."

It was a family belief that Judge Hiram Chrystal could solve anything. Even Alexander Chrystal believed in him. And sure enough, one phone call produced a solution. It was not, however, what Chelsea would have considered a good solution.

"The Halfway House," said the Judge. "We have funded a goodly portion of it to begin with. They have a vacancy now and we're considering a ward of the court for that space. But I can easily assign Monty there instead."

Chelsea flew apart, her beautiful face as contorted as her mother's had been. "No!" she shrieked. "I can't stand that. He'll be right here in town and *I'm* the one who'll have to deal with it. He'll hang out with Johnnie Pickett again and all that raunchy mill crowd, and get into God knows what, and he'll be bored, so he'll see what evil he can do at the high school. Don't ruin my life, too, Daddy. Send Monty as far away as you can, please, please!"

"Act your age!" screamed her father, pounding *his* fist on the desk.

"Daddy, don't you understand what is happening? *Nothing* is happening to Monty. He gets to pick up right where he left off. Mother and I are the ones who are going to be punished. *In public.*"

Chapter Three

"You realize, of course," Ryan Simpson said quietly, "that the Halfway House is adjacent to the country club."

Ian MacFarland did not care that much for Ryan, but they had grown up together, and they shared another, less pleasant, bond. Last summer both their houses had been robbed. Both believed the robberies had been committed by Monty Chrystal, after he caddied for their parents.

"Dad said Monty annoyed him by never handing over the right club," Ian said, "and Mom said Monty walked too slowly and they had to wait for him. Imagine, waiting for your own caddy. A week later we're visiting my cousins on Nantucket and somebody breaks in the pantry window and vandalizes the place."

Ryan nodded. "At our house, he also — "

Ryan broke off. Chelsea Chrystal was walking toward them. Dressed in very bright clothing, she was as vivid in the dark school halls as a parrot in a dim jungle. Her short, sleek hair was a helmet of spun gold, and the laugh that pealed out was as musical as a flute.

Ryan Simpson loved Chelsea. He had loved her from childhood, and had vague plans of marrying her one day. But Monty was home. Or at least back in town. And that changed everything. Because now Ryan had to remember that Chelsea was related to this punk, had the same blood and the same genes.

Halfway House. Next to the golf club where people like Ryan and Ian's parents had yelled at Monty, refused to tip Monty, accused Monty of vandalizing their homes. Wonderful. It was easy to be charitable about Halfway House when the kids dumped there were strangers with family difficulties. But a known arsonist with imagined grudges against Chrystal Falls?

Ryan felt his skin crawl. With difficulty he smiled at Chelsea.

Josh Newhouse, standing slightly behind Ryan and Ian, observed Chelsea with a new appreciation. Of course Chels was beautiful, and he'd always admired the swathe she cut through school, but now he knew she had guts, too. She never batted an eye when the vicious gossip about her brother surfaced. She trod a very fine line between being loyal to Monty and admitting that Monty had made mistakes in the past.

He and his sister Dawn had not heard much about Monty. Chrystal Falls was a hotbed of gossip, so in a way this was surprising, but on the other hand, so much had happened since they had moved to town that nobody but Karen had mentioned a delinquent hundreds of miles away.

There was not a good comparison between the agony he'd felt at his father's death and the agony Chelsea must feel over her brother's return, but still, Josh felt he could understand emotional pain. He wondered who Chelsea would talk it over with. Certainly not Perky, who was the blabbermouth of the county. Probably not to his sister Dawn, who, though growing closer to Chelsea all the time, had a tendency to get too emotional over other people's problems. Chelsea wouldn't want anybody to weep and moan with her. She was too independent for that.

"Hi, boys," said Chelsea gaily. Her smile darted forth, as teasingly as always. They were like her court: Ian, who was merely courteous; Ryan, who had worshipped her forever; and Josh, who was beginning to.

They grinned at her uneasily. The forbidden topic was on their tongues and they could think of nothing else to say.

There was never silence around Chelsea.

She liked talk and laughter. But they couldn't give it to her, and she couldn't seem to start it herself. They stood frozen in the hall, without speaking. It was very awkward.

Chelsea said finally, "I know. You're uptight about Monty. But not as uptight as we are! At least he's semi-locked up, right? Curfew, yard chores, all that." She tacked a smile on her face — so different from her usual carefree, on-top-of-the-world smile. "Meanwhile, we have more interesting things to do than worry about his academic standing, right?"

But she didn't say what the interesting things were. She stood like a run-down music box. Josh said over the shoulders of Ian and Ryan, "We sure do. Like ice cream."

"Winter," said Ryan. "Too cold for ice cream."

"It is never too cold for ice cream," said Josh categorically. "Anyway, I have in mind ice cream at the hospital."

"The hospital?" the others repeated incredulously.

"I hang out there a lot," explained Josh, "what with waiting for my mother and all. Their peach ice cream is perfection. Chelsea here has been yearning for it for months."

"I've told you so at least a hundred times," said Chelsea, circling Ian and Ryan to reach Josh. She had never heard of hospital ice cream, seriously doubted that hospital ice cream was worth mentioning, let alone eating,

40

but she loved to flirt. She and Josh pretended they had had secret plans all winter to go to the hospital cafeteria and stoke up on peach ice cream.

Flirting was her favorite activity. She set fears of her brother aside and enjoyed herself with Josh. Watching Ryan's concern and confusion was a nice addition to the scene.

"When are you going to New York for your dress?" said Ryan.

You had to bring that up, didn't you? thought Chelsea. Just when I'm having fun for the first time since Monty got back, you had to throw in the dress. I've got a mother who doesn't want to leave the house. I don't know when I'm going to New York.

She did not allow herself to think, I don't know *if* I'm going to New York.

Dawn came running lightly up the hall to join them. She hugged her brother. A stab of jealousy went through Chelsea. I couldn't hug my brother, she thought. I don't even look at him if I can help it.

She considered Josh. What did he mean by peach ice cream? Did he mean peach ice cream? Or did he mean hugs, kisses, dates — and the Crystal Mall gala?

"Did I hear you talking about dresses?" said Dawn. She was determinedly bright, obviously not going to let recent gossip about Monty Chrystal interfere with a good day. "I've been shopping for days, Chels, and there

41

isn't much around. What with junior prom and senior prom only a few months off, and graduation and weddings and all, the dresses are already gone from the stores. You are so lucky you're going to New York."

What if we don't go to New York? thought Chelsea. What if I really don't have anything special to wear?

She, Chelsea Chrystal.

Ordinary.

Because of Monty.

Ryan said, "It doesn't matter where Chels goes for a dress. She'd look perfect in rags." He smiled gallantly at Chelsea.

Chelsea felt like kicking him. I would as soon move to Saudi Arabia as dress in rags, she thought. And I am not going to wear rags or anything ordinary to the opening of Chrystal Mall. I am going to glitter like the prisms and the fountains, when I dance with the governor. I'm going to be a princess, and that's that. She said to Josh, "That ice cream is melting."

Josh said, "Can't have that." He offered her his arm.

Ryan gave an inarticulate mutter. Ian raised his eyebrows. Chelsea took the arm, turned it into a rather intimate embrace, and sauntered down the hall without bothering to say good-bye to anybody.

Josh will take me to the ball, she thought. He'll be my prince. He's already my knight in shining armor, rescuing me from a conversation that was bound to turn to Monty.

Chelsea turned to Josh, ready to dazzle him. She would knock his socks off. She would make his heart skip beats. She would have him in the palm of her hand, the way she'd always had Ryan.

They drove to the hospital without talking much.

The cafeteria was filled with strange people. Every height, weight, race, uniform, deformity, and level of education sat at chipped formica tables on unstable metal chairs with scarred plastic seats. Chelsea never associated with crowds like this. She felt most odd standing in line with such a weird assortment of people — janitors and dieticians, surgeons and flower ladies, expectant mothers and sadly afflicted children. The ice cream, obviously homemade, was filled with great chunks of peach, and Josh bought two big dishes for each of them, and led her to a tiny window table where they were slightly out of the crush of humanity.

She took her white plastic spoon in her hand and looked at Josh before trying her first bite.

Thick, unruly hair. Profile a little too bony, a little too broad for symmetry. That Newhouse look that his mother and sister shared; you just knew this was a decent family, a good family. *Kind.*

His hand was very large, and oddly knotted.

She thought of it wrapped around a tennis racket, and thought of it wrapped around her, and she looked into his dark eyes and it happened.

She, Chelsea Chrystal, the most self-possessed, controlled member of her clan, fell for Josh Newhouse like a tree in a lightning storm. His presence overwhelmed her. She could scarcely even breathe.

The ice cream seemed miles below her spoon. She stared at him, thinking, *Josh, Josh.*

She didn't want cold ice cream.

She wanted warm love, warm touch, warm kisses.

Josh said, "Go on. Try it. It's not half bad."

His voice was light and teasing, and it referred to ice cream. Chelsea, shivering slightly, said, "All right," and she tried some ice cream. She thought, Oh, let's not sit here in this strange place eating ice cream! Let's go park somewhere.

She had never felt this way about a boy. She enjoyed Ryan, but he didn't mean that much to her and neither did his kisses. She had dated other boys, but more in order to have a good-looking escort than because she was crazy about the boy.

Crazy, thought Chelsea.

Her mind really did feel fragmented. She could hardly listen to Josh. She kept spooning the ice cream into her mouth and telling him, yes, it really was fine peach ice cream, and he kept talking to her, she thought they were hospital stories, but she couldn't seem to hear the words. Her heart was beating everywhere; the sounds of that pounding filled her mind and ears.

When it was her turn to talk, she had nothing to say.

She, Chelsea, nervous, tongue-tied, and inarticulate.

It was impossible.

It was like thinking of herself dressed in rags.

She didn't do this kind of thing. It was *Josh* who was supposed to get nervous, tongue-tied, and inarticulate, while she stayed in total control.

This is it, thought Chelsea Chrystal. This is love. I didn't know it would make me dizzy. I thought it would be something I could hold, like a box. Instead it's something that holds me.

She took her eyes off Josh for a moment — to rest them, as if looking at him was exhausting — and glanced around the cafeteria. The people no longer looked strange or threatening, but friendly and nice. She had a sense that they were all in a lifeboat together, all trying to survive, and that she liked them.

Can they see? she thought. Do they know? Is there an aura surrounding me? *Woman in love?*

She looked back at Josh. There was no aura

around him. There was a tall, dark, good-looking boy, telling a story she had forgotten to listen to. If he was in love with her, it didn't show.

How will I know? thought Chelsea. Will I have to ask?

She knew Josh. The Newhouse family was tough, but caring. Like Dawn, Josh was gentle, generous, thoughtful.

She had never met a better person.

She thought, Monty could destroy this. I must not let Monty know that I have found the man I'm going to love. I don't think Monty would hurt Josh, but I know he would hurt what is between us.

So it has to be a secret.

Love. It will have to be something in a box after all. Closed off and private. Safe from Montgomery Chrystal.

Chapter Four

When her brother had taken off with Chelsea, Dawn abandoned the rest to find Pete. He was, in his half-cooperative way, waiting for her. He was near a side exit, where he was almost invisible, and where he could easily slip off to his car — but also where she could find him if she tried.

She felt a familiar thrill on seeing him. There was a roughness to Pete that attracted her very much. She never quite knew if she had Pete or not. He was always on the verge of annoyance with her, always half ready to walk. It meant that every time they were together she was faintly nervous, and the nervousness contributed somehow to her feeling for Pete and made it all the more exciting.

"Hi," she said breathlessly, and this time he grinned carelessly, swung her around with his strong, muscular arm, and kissed her hard. Dawn was delighted — and also aware that there were no witnesses. Once again the interest in her was controlled. Pete could only let it show in private. Dawn resented that a little. It seemed to her if you really liked someone, you were proud of it. You showed it off. You displayed it.

But she said nothing, and they walked out to Pete's car. It was hardly even a car, just an auto body on wheels. Dawn didn't even like getting into it, because it was rusty and the seats were torn, but Pete had paid for it, and paid the insurance, and paid for the gas and oil. Therefore he didn't notice the rust and the tears, because he had worked so hard to earn the money for the rest of it.

"I'm bad, Pete," she said to him as he started the motor.

He was startled for a moment and then laughed. "Yeah? Tell me about it. Sounds interesting. Has potential."

"Don't tease me when I'm being serious. We haven't talked about anything all day except buying a dress for the ball."

"*I* haven't talked about buying a dress for the ball," said Pete. "I haven't even *thought* about buying a dress for the ball."

"Oh, shut up. I'm serious."

"I love you when you're serious."

"Don't condescend to me, Pete Carter!" she snapped.

48

He quit teasing and nodded. "Sorry. Why are you bad?" Then he couldn't help himself and laughed anyhow. Dawn didn't have a bad blood cell, let alone bad habits or thoughts.

"I'm throwing away money on a gown when people are starving in Ethiopia," she said.

"There are probably a few people starving in Chrystal Falls, too," said Pete. "What are you going to do for their hunger? Give them a pair of satin dancing shoes?"

"Pete, you're not paying attention to me. Now listen to what I'm saying." She glared at him.

Pete Carter took his eyes off the road to catch the glare and it shocked him slightly. He loved teasing Dawn because she always rose to the teasing. But she really was mad at him, and it shook him a little. He had walked away from her more than once — but he suddenly realized she might walk away from him. Here he was wrapped up in teasing, while she was totally serious.

He decided he felt more like laughing than getting into a heavy talk about Justice On Earth, so he teased her anyway. "I'm listening."

"I'm a sponge," said Dawn. "It's time I contributed something to this world instead of taking."

"Good idea. Contribute a little to my sex life, okay? I think a good start would be — "

"Pete!" she said.

"I'm being serious, just like you told me. Sex is just as basic a need of mankind as food."

"You keep teasing me, Pete Carter, and you're going to starve for that, too."

"Oh," said Pete. "Okay. Then I won't tease."

He got such a kick out of her company. First of all, she was a lovely girl — smart, pretty, funny, good company. Second, however, she was a Hill girl — rich, doctor's daughter, country club. At the same time Pete disapproved of associating with snobs and effete tennis types, he also got a charge out of seeing the expressions on the faces of people like Chelsea Chrystal and Ryan Simpson when he, Pete, son of the union organizer, moved into their territory so easily.

Dawn said, "Drive past the Halfway House, will you, Pete?" She thought, I have to do something. I never worried about money and position and life until I came to Chrystal Falls. This mill town is so divided it automatically divides your thoughts. "I think," she added slowly, "that that's where I'll volunteer. Mrs. Chrystal volunteers there, did you know that?"

Pete nearly missed the turn in the road. "She *used* to," he said sharply. "Doesn't now. Monty's there. You don't know Monty, Dawn. You don't *want* to know Monty."

She smacked her hands down on her stack of school books. "Oh, honestly!" cried Dawn. "I am so sick of this nasty gossip. The only thing people in this town ever do is say bad things about each other."

"But there isn't anything you *can* say about Monty except bad things," protested Pete.

"You have a grudge against him because he's a Chrystal," Dawn accused him. "So he's wild. Lots of boys are wild. You aren't exactly the type to sit home and embroider, yourself, Pete Carter. And if Monty had committed any real crimes, he'd be in jail now."

Pete was stung. "Life doesn't work out fairly!" he retorted. "People like Monty Chrystal can slip out from under things. And I don't dislike him because he's a rich Chrystal. I dislike him because he's slime."

Dawn whirled on him. "A brother of Chelsea's could never be slime," she said fiercely. "Mrs. Chrystal wouldn't allow it."

"I can't believe you could say anything so stupid," was Pete's sharp answer. "Bad people pop up in all families, just the way good people do. Mitch Boyd is the only decent person in his family. Well, in the Chrystal clan, Monty is the dirt."

He stopped. Dawn was looking at him with a combination of anger and disgust. It was just the way he was feeling toward her, and he couldn't bear those destructive emotions between them. All because of the Chrystals!

51

Pete wanted to tell her about the suspected arson and robberies, but there had never been proof. If he talked about it, she'd demand proof, and when he couldn't produce any, she'd accuse him of hating Monty just because he was rich.

As for Mrs. Chrystal "not allowing" her son to be bad — that really was a stupid remark. Monty was six feet tall and a hundred eighty pounds and what his mother wanted did not interest Monty. He'd as soon insult his mother as look at her. And here was Dawn assuming anybody who drove a Mercedes and went to prep school was automatically decent.

"You didn't turn in," said Dawn irritably. "Turn around and go back into the Halfway House driveway."

"Don't order me around!" snapped Pete. Now what? he thought miserably. If I keep going and take her to McDonald's, she'll say I'm trying to push her around. If I turn around and take her to Halfway House, I'll be giving in to very poor judgment on her part.

He looked at her. The normally sweet profile was lifted in anger and turned away from him. *Oh, Dawn,* he thought. You really know how to complicate a guy's feelings.

Frustration went right to his feet. He pressed the accelerator at the same time as he swung a U-turn. Tires screaming, he took a very dangerous cross-traffic circle, panicking a half-dozen cars and terrifying Dawn. Pete was rather disappointed. He'd half hoped for a cop to see him and pull him over, so he could yell at the cop. He couldn't yell at Dawn again.

The trouble with Dawn was that she aroused so much tension in him. The uncertainty he always felt around her was magnified by her stupid desire to volunteer at Halfway House. Why couldn't she deliver flowers at the hospital or make phone calls for the Cancer Drive or something reasonable like that? No, she had to go to a place where Monty Chrystal would be hanging around.

The driveway was badly rutted. Stones jarred the tires, and winter-hardened earth, like iron, slowed Pete's speed. Heavy, ugly shrubbery lined the drive too thickly. Escape-proof, thought Pete, eyeing the thorns. Blue spruce had grown as blue spruce does: overpowering the house, pushing darkly up against its windows, and shading the lawn so that nothing green could ever grow there.

It was sinister, and he was glad. He could detect Dawn's apprehension. Maybe she wouldn't come to a place as unpleasant as this.

But behind the Halfway House the personality of the place changed entirely. A wide lawn stretched in the weak winter sun. A glassed-in porch was bright with hanging plants. Two young boys were practicing basketball, shouting, hustling, leaping happily. An older couple, obviously the house parents, were painting a yard chair — although it was pretty early in the season for that — and a painfully thin teenager with a complexion that needed sunshine was making an effort to be helpful but just getting in the way.

When Pete parked the car, all of them turned and smiled.

Nice smiles, from nice people.

Another boy, perhaps fourteen or so, wearing a torn windbreaker over faded jeans, emerged from the back door, carrying an enormous wooden bowl filled with potato chips and a pint of sour cream straight out of the refrigerator. Immediately the four boys descended on their treat and the chips began to vanish into the bottomless pits of their stomachs. The house parents grinned.

Dawn slid out of the car, the house parents walked in a welcoming way to greet her, and Pete's heart sank even lower. This would appeal to Dawn: the nice people struggling to make a happy home in difficult surroundings. "I'm Dawn Newhouse," she said, and he heard excitement in her voice and cringed.

The house parents were Mr. and Mrs. Sheffield. Unwillingly, Pete got out of the car to meet them, too. He knew Dawn would be even more annoyed by him if he stayed there, surly and uncooperative.

In fact, the Sheffields needed someone to

tutor one of their boys. "Gideon is twelve," they told Dawn. "His parents moved so often Gideon went to two or three schools a year, and he's never really learned to read at all. We'd be so grateful to someone who'd help Gideon with his reading two or three afternoons a week."

"I'm Gideon," said one of the scrawny basketball players shyly. Teeth that needed braces, glasses that needed washing, hair that needed a trim. Even Pete was touched. The boy looked so abandoned! A quick glance at Dawn told him she had found the volunteer work she wanted: a boy obviously in need, obviously eager for help.

His anger at her vanished, to be replaced by an intense surge of love. How many girls cared so much for the downtrodden? Did he even know another girl who would want to save Gideon, let alone the world?

He loved her for caring.

He stood by her, and as the Sheffields and Gideon talked, his hand found her waist, slowly circled it, and settled there, claiming Dawn, telling all these people that this lovely, decent girl was his, and his alone.

Karen could not find Mitch after school.

It surprised her, because Mitch liked to wait for her. She drove to his house on A Avenue, six blocks from her own, because she felt like talking, but his car wasn't there. No point talking to Mitch's family. They neither knew nor cared where Mitch was.

She went home alone and did her homework while she watched soap operas on television. She'd been too busy for weeks to see any afternoon television and she was lost; everybody was into some other kind of difficulty now.

Mitch had been keeping something from her all week. It was not like him. He was usually like a puppy wagging his tail around Karen and he told her everything. What could there be that he would hide from her? It made Karen anxious.

The Picketts had supper and Karen had finished the dishes and put most of them away when Mitch walked in the back door. He didn't knock. He was all but a son of the family anyhow. Karen was so relieved to see him. How solid he was! Not a weakling in spirit like Ryan Simpson, nor a well-dressed preppy like Ian MacFarland, but a hard-working, decent, kind boy. I love him, she thought. I wish that he had more ambition. I wish that he wanted to be a go-getter. I wish I thought he planned to leave Chrystal Falls and find something better.

But I love him.

She crossed the kitchen with the dish towel still in her hands and stopped before kissing him. "Wow, are you dirty!" she exclaimed. "What have you been up to?"

"I meant to go home and shower first, but I wanted to see you," he said. He had a breathless excitement in his face, and a little apprehension.

He's going to tell me something important, thought Karen. "It's a good thing I love you," she said, touching his dirt-streaked face. "This is a real test."

From under the grime came his wonderful wide smile. Her heart flipped. "Karen," he said quietly, "I'm quitting high school. Finelli offered me a full-time job and I'm taking it."

She thought that this time her heart would stop instead of flip. "No," she whispered. "No. Never. *Mitch!* You'll never get out of Chrystal Falls if you don't even have a high school diploma."

"I don't *want* to get out of Chrystal Falls," he said. "This is my home. Listen to me, Karen. Finelli hired a bunch of us — Pete and me and some others — to help clean up the new mall. It was just dump runs. Shoveling debris into trucks. But good pay. I was just doing it for the extra money. But here's what happened. A couple of the trucks broke down and I was able to fix them for Mr. Finelli. He was really impressed. He said I was already the best mechanic he'd come across in a long time and he'd like me on his payroll. Karen, it will be union wages. And when Finelli's done with the mall, he's going to do that airport expansion. It's a terrific opportunity. And he needs someone *now*."

Oh, no, thought Karen. Oh, God, please, no. Bad enough he wants to live in Chrystal Falls till the day he dies — but to quit school? "No," she said fiercely.

"Finelli needs me *now*," he answered her. "And as a mechanic for him, I'd earn a lot more than schoolteachers, or insurance salesmen, or any of those careers you think are nice. I'd — "

"No!" she screamed. She grabbed him by the unbuttoned edges of his filthy wool shirt and shook him. He was too big to shake. Only the shirt moved. "No, no, a thousand times no!" she screamed. "You can't do that!"

He had known this would happen. Karen believed in education the way some people believe in religion. "My education is going to be with engines and — "

"You're not quitting high school!" she screamed, stamping her foot.

"I'll be earning money," he pointed out. "When you go to college, I can pay your tuition. Easy."

"Why would you pay for it?" she demanded.

"Because we'll get married," he said confidently. "What you don't get in scholarships, I'll pay."

"I am not getting married the day I finish high school," she said.

Mitch tried to joke with her. "How about the day *after* you finish high school? That's

58

a Saturday anyhow. Better for a wedding than a Friday."

Karen stepped away from him. The hot flash of rage had gone. She stood quietly. "Mitch," she said. "I love you. But if you quit high school, you quit me, too."

Behind Pete a door slammed. He turned automatically at the sound of slapping wood. There on the back porch, framed against the dark of the interior, was Montgomery Chrystal. The only son and heir.

Shoulders back, pelvis thrust forward, Monty came very slowly down the four back steps. He glanced at Pete, sneered, and did not bother to speak. They had always hated each other. When Monty Chrystal was in third grade, Pete Carter was in first. Monty's specialty was beating up on little kids who couldn't fight back.

Pete Carter had always fought back. Always would.

He could still remember the principal's fury. Little Pete Carter from the mill had given a Chrystal a bloody nose. He still remembered the injustice of it all, that he, Pete, was punished, and Monty was soothed and hugged.

Pete's hand stayed protectively on Dawn's waist.

Pete wondered what had happened at the Maine prep school. Still no high school graduation. Would Monty be back at Chrystal Falls High with the rest of them? That would destroy a promising year in a hurry.

They'll probably make him join the Army, thought Pete.

Poor Army.

Dawn Newhouse turned to look at the broad-shouldered, dark boy who walked up to her. He was older than the other boys here, and he lacked that skinny vulnerability they had. He was mature. Arrogant.

Mr. and Mrs. Sheffield spoke to him almost warily.

It made Dawn look at the boy again. He was handsome in a rebellious, sulking way. He seemed too old to need a temporary home. She wondered what had brought him here.

The boy held out his hand for Dawn to shake. She took it, of course. His hand was much larger than Pete's. It enclosed her small fingers and held onto them, as if she were his prisoner. She looked up into his face. He was staring down at her with intense, strangely familiar eyes that raked through her clothing to her skin.

She shivered, not knowing if it was a shiver of fear.

When he spoke his voice was astonishingly deep. Gravel at the bottom of the pit. The voiced rasped over her senses. "Hello, Dawn," he said.

How had he known her name? He must have been standing by the door listening. She was oddly flattered and found herself blushing.

"I'm Monty Chrystal," he said.

This was Chelsea's renegade brother? But of course. The eyes. That same commanding self-assurance, although Chelsea's were bright blue and Monty's were a dark, unfathomable brown.

He did not let go of her hand.

Mr. Sheffield said, "What's the matter, Monty? Your fingers frozen?" He was laughing, but uncertainly.

They don't know how to handle a Chrystal, either, Dawn thought.

Monty laughed, too, and let go of her slowly. The laugh was as deep as his voice. Cellar laughter — bottom of the basement laughter.

She was every much aware of Pete standing next to her, of that possessive hand resting on her waist. Monty's eyes left hers and went to Pete's, and the two locked stares. It's a duel, thought Dawn. They're dueling over *me*.

And even though it was primitive and stupid, she loved it. The sense of territory that Pete was staking, the sense of Monty warning him he might invade — to her amazement, Dawn did not want to interfere. She wanted it to happen. Although they were much stronger than she, she was the powerful one, because they both wanted her.

Mrs. Sheffield said that Tuesday and Thursday afternoons would be convenient for Gideon to be tutored. Dawn said that would be good for her, too. Pete said, "Fine. Let's go, Dawn."

Dawn separated herself from him. She was not exactly sure why. I'm trying to tell Monty I don't necessarily belong to Pete Carter, even if Pete thinks so, she realized. How strange. I love Pete!

When Monty grinned good-bye, Dawn thought it a very sexy, exciting grin.

When Pete saw the same grin it reminded him of a snake.

Chapter Five

Sunday dinner at the Chrystals was traditionally held at the country club. Partly because the servants had Sunday off and partly because all their friends were there, and it was an effortless party.

But this Sunday they ate at home.

Monty was coming to dinner.

There was no way they could take him to the club. How could they put their friends in the awkward position of having to speak courteously to the boy they all believed had robbed them? And how could the Chrystals themselves glue falsely happy smiles on their faces all Sunday afternoon?

It was no day of rest for the Chrystals. It was a day of knotted anxiety.

Chelsea and her mother heated what the cook had prepared the evening before.

Monty's favorites. We always cater to him, thought Chelsea. Even now, when we all know it's too late and it's also wrong. Veal roast, wild rice, asparagus, braided bread, and chocolate mousse. Monty had always had very sophisticated tastes. He never wanted a hot dog. He preferred filet mignon.

Chelsea thought, He'll be okay. He'll never end up in prison where he belongs, and he'll always be able to afford the filet mignon, because my family will always pay him off instead of punishing him.

The dining room was breathtakingly beautiful. Filled with the flowers that were her mother's passion and lit by the low chandelier, the room was softly charming and warmly welcoming. Its air of elegance gone by, of belonging to another era, was no mistake. Elizabeth Chrystal's whole life was like that.

"I have a terrible headache," said Chelsea's mother, as they finished arranging the flowers.

Nobody was surprised. Her worst headaches invariably coincided with Monty's presence.

"He'll be here in a few minutes," said Alexander Chrystal heavily. "Perhaps you could take a few aspirin and at least manage to stay with us for the first course."

In the driveway they heard the soft purr of Grandfather Hiram's car, returning from Halfway House with Monty.

"Aspirin doesn't touch my headaches," said

Elizabeth. She looked almost frantically toward the door. She was beginning to pale.

Father and daughter exchanged silent looks. Alexander Chrystal looked very old. He shrugged and turned away. Chelsea said, "I'll walk you upstairs, Mother."

Her mother did not walk. She almost ran in her eagerness to be hidden before her son came into the house. She had not seen him since he had come back to Chrystal Falls. The thick carpet absorbed the sound of her light feet, and when the door of her bedroom closed, Chelsea was not surprised to hear the click of the lock.

Chelsea shivered.

Then she walked to the front door to say hello to her brother.

At the Gilberts' house, Dr. Barbara Newhouse, Josh, and Dawn were sitting down to a rack of lamb with Uncle Walt, Aunt Vicki, and their cousin Tim.

As long as Aunt Vicki kept her mouth shut, they could all get along wonderfully. Barbara and Walt told medical stories, Tim told college stories, and Josh told tennis stories. The table rang with laughter.

Aunt Vicki interrupted this flow. "Dawn," she said in her sharp voice, "we haven't heard much from you. What is going on in your life?" She managed to imply that nothing would be going on in Dawn's life. She had been annoyed by Dawn from the beginning because Dawn insisted on making friends — and keeping them — with the wrong people.

"I'm going to volunteer at the Halfway House, teaching a boy how to read," said Dawn.

"How wonderful, darling!" exclaimed her mother. "I'm so proud of you." At the same instant, her aunt cried, "Dawn, that is *unthinkable*. You may not do it."

"Don't be ridiculous," said Dr. Newhouse. "Volunteer work is always good. Dawn, I'm delighted with that decision."

Aunt Vicki pursed her brightly painted lips tightly. On anybody else, it was lipstick. On Aunt Vicki it was a garish slash of red paint. "This is stupidity," she snapped. "Halfway House is filled with nasty punks."

"If you're referring to Monty Chrystal," said Dawn, who had had enough of this argument with Pete, "then I think — "

If Aunt Vicki had had any sense of tact, she might have succeeded. But instead of hearing Dawn out she interrupted and said to Dr. Newhouse, "You've got to exercise more control over your children, Barbara. It is simply a disgrace the way you allow them to — "

"Vicki!" exclaimed Dr. Newhouse. "I will not get into a discussion with you on how to raise my children! I am very proud that Dawn has made this decision. *Other* girls are out there worrying about prom dresses and boyfriends, and *my* daughter is helping people. I think it's wonderful, and I'd like to close the subject if you're going to argue."

Naturally Aunt Vicki had no intention of closing the subject. It was a very meaty subject, with lots of potential, and she launched into a major fight with her sister-in-law.

Josh took a long sip of ice water. He hated water, wanted Coke, and hated lamb and would have preferred spaghetti. Why did they have to keep going to the Gilberts, when one third of the family was so horrible? He daydreamed about Chelsea instead. He could not remember when he had been so drawn to a girl. He liked girls and dated often, but never before had a single girl captivated him. Now Chelsea drifted in his mind's eye, and he felt as if he could touch her, hear her voice, see her sparkling blue eyes daring him on.

Now instead of being with Chelsea, he was wasting a good Sunday afternoon listening to Aunt Vicki's drivel.

At last Josh couldn't stand it anymore. Excusing himself on the pretense of getting more ice water, he slipped into the guest bedroom down the hall, picked up the extension, and called Chelsea's number.

Karen Pickett tested the temperature outdoors, found it was still definitely winter, and wore heavy clothes. She went to the tennis courts over by the junior high. She didn't really care for tennis, partly because it was so dominated by the country club set she detested, but today she felt like hitting something, and it was better to hit tennis balls than Mitch.

She didn't go over to the courts. She stood behind the junior high, whacking ball after ball against the two-story brick wall of the building. When the ball bounced back, she returned it with enough force, she felt, to burst it.

Mitch. Quitting high school.

The stupid, ignorant, short-sighted, worthless. . . .

Tears made it very hard to see the balls, even lime green balls.

Why, oh why, had she fallen in love with somebody like Mitch? She, Karen, who intended to dump Chrystal Falls like so much rubbish after her high school graduation, who meant to conquer the world — perhaps from Chicago, or New York, or Dallas, but *never* from this backwater mill town — she had to love this mechanic who wanted to live on A Avenue forever.

She had a dozen balls with her. She batted them fiercely, rounded them up, and whacked them again.

Of course, Mitch did have ambition. Just a different kind. He wanted a happy marriage with contented children. He wanted his car paid for and his meals hot. And he wanted Karen.

The thought of repeating her mother's life made her ill.

High school graduation was not that close, but to Karen it was the sign on the exit door: gleaming in the night, taking her out of town for good, into a better world.

And Mitch was quitting high school.

She stooped to pick up a lime green ball, and saw trousered legs next to her. Jumping awkwardly, frightened, she turned to see Mitch. Holding his windbreaker like an apron, he had gathered up all her tennis balls. He looked like an apple picker without a bushel basket.

They stared at each other.

"Don't be mad at me," said Mitch. " I can't stand it."

"I can't, either," whispered Karen. She flung herself on him, with as much energy as if she hadn't been hitting tennis balls for forty-five minutes. Mitch dropped the edges of his jacket and tennis balls spilled about their feet. They kissed with an intensity that sealed their love. She could not get enough of him. She hung onto him, her fingers in his hair, her hands around his neck. Their embrace was so tight it really felt as if nothing on earth could ever come between them.

"You win," said Mitch.

She drew back and looked at him.

He nodded. "I won't take the job. I told Finelli."

"What did he say?"

"He said to stick with you."

Karen laughed and hugged him fiercely. She was small but athletic: It was hug enough to make Mitch wince. "Best advice I've heard in years," she told him. Enough love beween us, thought Karen, gazing into Mitch's eyes, and maybe we really can conquer the world.

Mitch felt a passing disappointment for the job he had wanted, and a shade of despair at the thought of yet more school. But the pleasure in Karen's eyes meant a great deal.

He held her, and thought, okay for now . . . but was it right for me?

Chelsea, at least, knew it was right for her. "Oh, Josh!" she cried into the telephone. "I'm so glad to hear your voice. Everything here is absolutely awful."

"What's wrong?" said Josh. He was used to things being absolutely awful, but he couldn't stand the idea of Chelsea in that situation.

"My rotten brother is here. Making life miserable for all of us. My mother's hiding in her room. Last time Monty was home we hardly laid eyes on her for a month."

To Josh it was a heaven-sent opportunity. He didn't have to think of something exciting and unusual to entice Chelsea to go out with

70

him — he just had to be there. He said, "I'll pick you up and we'll go for a drive, how's that?"

For Chelsea, that was perfect. The thought of a few hours with Josh, who appealed to her more than any boy ever had, released her from a hundred worries. With a skill developed over a lifetime of dealing with Monty, she put Monty out of her mind. He wasn't worth the space.

Josh, on the other hand, was worth it all.

They teased each other over the phone, drawing out the conversation just to hear each other's voices.

There isn't another person in Chrystal Falls to equal him, thought Chelsea Chrystal. Maybe not in all Pennsylvania.

She giggled softly. Maybe not in the *world*.

Half an hour later the phone rang again for Chelsea Crystal. Ryan Simpson was lying beside his indoor swimming pool, thinking that Chelsea in a bathing suit would be just the right addition to a boring Sunday afternoon.

Chelsea had an exuberance that transferred to everyone around her. It was such a welcome thing that people followed her around even though she never attempted to lead. She just automatically attracted a crowd. But since her brother's return, Chelsea had been a little down. Ryan could hardly blame her. *He* was a little down about Monty's return, and he

71

didn't have to admit to being related to the creep.

. He would invite her over to have a little fun.

Chelsea loved the Simpson pool. Originally installed so Ryan's father could swim laps, it was a custom pool, very long, very narrow. Wide Mexican tiles surrounded it, and above it rose a peaked glass ceiling. The water, of course, was heated. In the humid room a jungle of tropical plants thrived. Vines and flowers climbed along the south side of the pool, and white rattan furniture hid in a nook formed by potted trees and hanging orchids, fuchsias, and ferns.

Chelsea had a bikini so small it didn't count.

"Wear your bikini," ordered Ryan, smiling into the telephone.

"Can't come over," said Chelsea. "I'm busy, darling. Maybe another time."

She didn't sound upset at all, even though he knew Monty had been taken from Halfway House for dinner. Chelsea actually sounded happy. "Monty being sent off so soon?" he guessed.

Her voice darkened. "Don't talk to me about Monty. No, I have other plans."

No explanation.

Ryan said, "Yeah? Like what? Homework?"

There was a tiny pause, in which she considered whether to tell him. "I'm just going out," she said, leaving it at that, and Ryan was furious. So she had something better to do, with some*one* better. He tried to end the conversation easily, but he couldn't manage it. "With Josh?" he said, before he could stop himself.

"With Josh," agreed Chelsea, coolly.

She hung up first, and then Ryan slammed the phone down. All the phones in the Simpson house rang in protest against this violence.

Ryan stormed out of the house. Whenever he was furious he liked to drive fast. It made him feel better to put the pedal to the metal.

Swearing, he found his own car blocked by both his parents' cars. Fury rose even higher in Ryan. He could, of course, switch all the cars around. That would take fifteen minutes, he thought. In this mood he'd probably pretend he was in a demolition derby and smash all the fenders on purpose.

Ryan's father in a bad mood was a lot worse to deal with than Ryan in a bad mood.

So Ryan just took his mother's car. She didn't like large cars and liked parallel parking even less, so hers was a tiny subcompact with automatic that Ryan and his father referred to as "the tricycle," because it hardly deserved the name car. Ryan rarely drove it. When he got out on the road, he found it had so little power that even when he did put the pedal to the floor, nothing happened.

He circled the country club. It was very

chilly, very windy, and still winter, but die-hard golfers thought any day without snow was a golfing day. Just as Ryan Simpson drove past the shared lot-line where Halfway House lurked behind its overgrown blue spruces, the long, impressive CRSTL I Mercedes belonging to Judge Hiram Chrystal slowly entered the rutted drive. Monty was in the backseat.

Ryan slowed to a crawl, which was easy in the tricycle. It liked crawling. Ryan had always been a little afraid of Monty Chrystal. Now, just to increase Ryan's terrible mood, Monty saw him. In this stupid excuse for a car.

Monty laughed at him. Ryan could figure out that laugh through both cars' windows, across the road. Hard, taunting eyes greeted Ryan.

The Mercedes vanished into the thick, ugly shrubbery.

Ryan felt like running Monty over. It would do the world a lot of good. Of course, in this stupid little pretend car, Monty probably wouldn't even get a bruise. Just pick up the car like a Tonka toy and throw it away.

Ryan, unable to deal with his anger by driving fast, took his alternate route. He made his way to The Strip, and entered a bar. Lying about his age, he had a beer. And then he had another.

* * *

As for Chelsea, she, too, would have liked to run Monty over, but when Josh arrived, she was too delighted to bother. Why waste a wonderful afternoon talking about her loser brother? Besides, she really didn't want Josh to know the details. When Josh, being courteous, asked her about Monty, she shrugged, laughing easily. "I was exaggerating," she told him. "It's no big deal. So, what'll we do this afternoon?" She settled herself on the passenger side of Josh's car. She took her time doing it, so he would watch her.

He forgot about Monty as quickly as she had intended him to.

Chelsea was a happy girl and she craved happiness around her. Given a chance, she would be cheerful, never melancholy. She could not imagine being like her mother, and holing up with her anxieties. Chelsea would fling them away and find something to enjoy.

"Let's go bowling," said Josh.

She couldn't believe her ears. *"Bowling?"* she said. "Josh, don't be ridiculous."

"What's ridiculous about it?"

"Josh, I don't bowl."

"Time you learned," he said, and headed the car toward The Strip.

Chelsea so rarely had business on this side of town that driving The Strip was something of an adventure in itself. It wasn't a bad area — fast food places, income tax chains, discount shoes, bars, bowling alleys — but it was as forbidden to Chelsea as crime. She looked out the window, as if they were driving in another country.

When you get excited driving past a tire store, she thought, giggling at herself, you know it's time for a change.

"How come you never learned to bowl?" said Josh.

"I don't know. It's sort of a — well, you just don't bowl at the country club, Josh. Bowling is a — well, I don't want to be a snob — but it's a — "

Josh grinned. "A low class sport," he supplied. "Mill hands join bowling leagues. Chrystals play polo."

Chelsea giggled. "I've never even seen a polo match in my life."

"Oh, well, then, that's what we'll do next Sunday. Play polo. You do have a string of polo ponies, don't you?"

"Oh, of course," said Chelsea. "We keep them at the stable on the off chance our guests might want a little game."

Josh patted her knee. She wanted his hand to stay there. "I love bowling," said Josh. "I'm no good at it. They try to throw me out because I'm dangerous to the health of the floor, but I love it. So I'm going to teach you how."

Chelsea felt as if she were slumming. Nobody, but nobody, from the Hill went bowling. It was a very popular mill-hand activity. There were enough leagues that people working day, swing, or night shift could all participate at any level of expertise. It was unthinkable that a Chrystal would play along with them.

But Chelsea loved anything new, and this was definitely new. Besides, it was with Josh, and anything with Josh was a good thing.

She unfastened her seat belt and moved closer to him. He took one hand off the wheel and put it around her. Safety was such a byword in her family that she felt like a sinner just taking off the seat belt. She could think of nothing but Josh. He was wearing a heavy coat. She could not really be close to him no matter how close she sat, because of the padding he wore.

Josh talked about school and a project for history he didn't feel like doing. Chelsea thought, I'll ask him to go with me to the Chrystal Mall gala. We'll be perfect together.

She meant it. She was perfect, Josh was perfect, and life, if she could get rid of Monty, would also be perfect.

Chelsea smiled happily. She snuggled against Josh. She did not see Ryan Simpson come out of the bar, look into the Newhouse vehicle, and recognize the two of them. Every time she had driven with Ryan, she had stayed calmly on the passenger side, tucked in by her seat belt, quite a distance from Ryan as he drove. Chelsea didn't know that nothing in this whole infuriating day had infuriated Ryan Simpson more than seeing Chelsea Chrystal without her seat belt, snuggled up to Josh Newhouse.

Chapter
Six

It was very much a Monday morning. People dragged themselves down the corridors and dropped like sacks of sand into their chairs. Eyes half focused, they half listened in class.

Only Mitch Boyd was enthusiastic and excited. In spite of all the conflict, he had had a great weekend. During free period, he went down to the student center, hoping to find Karen, but she was evidently spending the hour in the library. Chelsea was leaning against one of the marble pillars. Who had a better right? Her grandfather had had the student center built thirty years ago.

Somewhat to his surprise, she initiated a conversation with him. They were not exactly close. "I hear you're working on my mall," drawled Chelsea.

He had to laugh. Good thing Karen hadn't heard that. If Karen hated "getting my dress in New York, of course," she would *really* hate "working on *my* mall."

"Pete and I got temporary jobs cleaning up," he agreed. "There's a lot of debris after a construction job. We were running around with our wheelbarrows and our shovels, choking on the dust."

"It's only a month until completion," protested Chelsea. "How can you still be using wheelbarrows to cart away the mess? You should be polishing and scouring by now."

"Maybe you should come by and supervise," said Mitch. "Be sure to tell everybody you think they should be moving along faster."

"Okay, okay, I'm sorry. I'm just surprised. I thought the heavy stuff would be done."

He relented. "Mostly it is. But there's no point in cleaning up until everybody is done. Now almost everybody is done."

"Is the crystal chandelier up yet?"

There was to be one enormous chandelier, as big, people said, as a room. "No," Mitch told her. "Guess they're waiting until the pounding and hammering is over. But the fountain is finished."

Chelsea clapped her hands. "Tell me about it!"

He liked her excitement. "It's got thick slabs of glass cantilevered out over each other like pieces breaking off a glacier," he said. "Under the water the tile is a deep royal blue. There are stars worked into the tiles. And — "

Perky Palmer had come up to join Chelsea. Perky interrupted Mitch rather sharply. "Is the water turned on yet?" she demanded. Perky always managed to make an ordinary sentence obnoxious. Mitch just looked at her. Normally Perky wouldn't be caught dead talking to Mitch, but she was as interested in the magnificent new mall as anyone. Perhaps more so. Shopping was one of the few skills Perky had.

"Where will the dancing be?" said Chelsea, without caring if he answered Perky.

"I guess around the fountain. There's a lot of open space. Teak benches. Island for ferns and plants. The floor is brick. It's laid in radiating circles that interlock and spread. Like ripples on a pond. And on the walls, where the sunlight comes through the prisms that hang from the top story, there are rainbows."

"A poet," observed Perky. "English class really took with you, didn't it, Mitch? Shame you're just going to spend your life rebuilding transmissions."

Mitch just nodded. "What are *you* going to do that's useful?" he asked mildly.

But it was the wrong word. Perky didn't have to worry about being "useful" and to her it was just another indication of the gap between Hill and Mill — that this heavy-handed jerk would even think such a thing.

They stood awkwardly. Chelsea broke the silence, saying, "Do you think it'll be done by deadline, Mitch?"

"Seventeen days?" He shrugged. "Guess so. Nobody at the site is worried, anyhow."

"Seventeen days?" gasped Chelsea Chrystal. Mitch could have sworn she paled. But he had no chance to observe her more carefully. Perky linked a sharp elbow through Chelsea's and led her off. Mitch didn't miss them. They weren't worth much compared to his Karen.

Perky said, "When are we going to New York anyway? Seventeen days is cutting it pretty fine, Chels."

Chelsea was having a panic attack. Seventeen days was nearly impossible. What if her dress had to be altered? What if they couldn't find the right shoes? What if it took two trips to New York? What if —

"What's the matter, Chels?" demanded Perky, narrowing her eyes and staring in Chelsea's face.

Chelsea detesting admitting to anyone that anything was the matter. She loved being the princess, for whom all things came naturally and easily. Bad enough she should have to deal with everybody wondering about Monty. They weren't going to wonder whether she'd have any clothes for the dance. "I forgot to do my math," she lied.

Perky laughed. "Just lie to Mr. Kraft. He always believes you. I think he might even have a crush on you."

"Don't be silly," said Chelsea.

She pictured that brick floor Mitch described. Dusty red bricks, spreading like ripples on a pond. Herself in a gown that shimmered, with hair that gleamed and earrings that glittered. Wearing her grandmother Lillian's magnificent emerald and diamond necklace, the one that had not been taken from the safe since the last family wedding. Tiny slippers to fit her narrow feet, darting gracefully out from under her floor-length skirt.

She would have to see that the band played a lot of fast stuff, as well as the slow, boring melodies of her parents' generation. She would have preferred a disk jockey, actually, but this was unthinkable to her parents and grandparents, whose lives had been built around big bands, and to whom a real celebration meant live music.

Josh. His life was simple. If he didn't own a tuxedo, he'd walk down to the store and rent a perfect one.

Josh was perfect anyhow. Tall and lean and dark and smiling down at her: intense and happy and proud to be with her. Chelsea giggled at the thought of their dreadful bowling scores. They had laughed so much together they barely managed to hoist the balls, let alone keep them out of the gutters and score.

Seventeen days. That was only two weeks. She had had no idea that time was moving so quickly. Monty coming back home had thrown her off schedule. She had to rush home this afternoon and get her mother moving along, making plans for the New York trip.

"Hi, there," said Ryan Simpson, catching up to her. "So how's life, kid?"

Perky, who was a tiny bit jealous that Ryan was Chelsea's puppy, knew that Ryan wasn't bothering to ask *her* how life was. She thought, Chels will go to the ball with Ryan. And who will *I* go with?

"Wonderful, thanks," said Chelsea, omitting great portions that were lousy.

"You're practically dancing down the hall."

"That's because I'm thinking about the gala at the Chrystal Mall."

"That reminds me," began Ryan.

Immediately Chelsea knew she had said the wrong thing. She'd given Ryan an opening to ask her to go with him. She had no intention of being with anybody but Josh. Nor did she like the way Perky was watching them, eagerly, lapping it up. She liked her love life in private.

"The real problem," she told them both, "is my dress. I keep changing my mind about colors. Sometimes I want a pale, pale color.

Peach or barely pink. I love pastels. But other times I want something really splashy. I want to be reflected in every mirror the way the stars in the fountain will reflect in the water."

"What do you think?" teased Ryan. "You think you're some kind of star?"

"I *know* I am. And therefore I have to look the part. Mitch just told us the interior of the fountain pool is bright royal blue. Maybe that's the color I should go with. Well, here we are at English class! Have a nice day, Ryan." She walked into class before he could utter another syllable. She was pleased with herself. She hadn't put him in a spot, she hadn't revealed anything in front of Perky, and she'd kept him from asking her to the gala.

And in this class, there was Josh to look at.

He was there, his eyes fixed on her already.

Chelsea loved that. Walking into a room and having the one person you wanted to think about be thinking about you.

"Hi, Josh," she said softly. She slipped into the seat next to him, marveling that such an ordinary greeting could bring such smiles from each of them.

Dawn spent her free period in the library. "Mrs. Finelli," she said to the librarian, "I'm going to be tutoring a twelve-year-old boy who can't read. How should I start?"

Mrs. Finelli loved to be asked for information. Filing, typing, shelving — that was a bore. But advice and information — she was overjoyed.

"Quite a few kids never learn to read. There are two possible reasons. The first is something wrong. Make sure he isn't dyslexic and doesn't need glasses. If that's not the problem, then probably the child has never found any reason to read. So before you teach him to read, you have to give him a reason to learn."

"Getting good grades?" suggested Dawn.

"Kids who don't read don't care about their grades," said Mrs. Finelli. "What I mean is, suppose you find that your boy loves wrestling."

Dawn shuddered.

"You borrow wrestling magazines from me. He'll love the pictures and he'll want to learn how to read the captions under them. He'll want to figure out the classified ads and send for stuff."

"Maybe he'll like fashion magazines," said Dawn.

She and Mrs. Finelli laughed. "Here," said the librarian. "Try these hobby and car magazines for a start."

Pete Carter found her fifteen minutes later, sitting Indian-style in front of magazines on model airplanes, model trains, stamps, coins, cars, white water rafting, and ham radio. "You going to collect pocket knives or beer cans?" asked Pete, squatting down beside her.

She told him about Mrs. Finelli's suggestion.

"I like Mrs. Finelli," said Pete. "She probably knows what she's talking about. Mitch and I've been working for Mr. Finelli the last few days. He's a good guy. Offered Mitch a permanent job."

"I can't imagine anything less interesting than construction," said Dawn. "Unless it's wrestling. I hope Gideon likes something I like. If we end up browsing through wrestling magazines . . . ugh."

"That reminds me," said Pete, snapping his fingers. "I got us a pair of front row tickets for a big wrestling match at the coliseum next week. Three-hundred-pound guys that wear fifty pounds of chains and a half ounce of clothes."

Dawn looked at Pete in horror.

Pete said innocently, "I never told you wrestling is my first love?"

"*I'm* your first love," said Dawn. She wasn't sure of this at all, and would never have said it if the two of them were being serious, but when they were teasing in the library, anything went.

Pete grinned, but whether the grin was agreement that she was his first love, or enjoyment of the repartee, Dawn did not know.

"What *do* you want to do this weekend?"

he said, although until now he hadn't said he wanted to do anything with her at all. "It's supposed to be warm and clear. Have you ever driven up into the real mountains north of us? It makes a nice trip and I'm kind of stir crazy after such a long winter."

"Back where I used to live they called it cabin fever," said Dawn.

"Good name. I've got it bad."

The bell rang. Dawn scooped up her magazines and gave Pete a quick kiss on the cheek, but he was getting to his feet at the same instant and his face left her lips. She got him on the side of the nose.

"Now I feel lopsided," said Pete. "Get the other side, too, will you?" Dawn kissed him so that he would feel symmetrical.

"When do you tutor Gideon?" asked Pete.

"Tomorrow."

He nodded, trying not to show his worry. He was being overly protective and he knew it. The Sheffields would be there. And Dawn wasn't stupid. She could take care of herself.

But as they parted Pete stared after her. He was not really sure of that. She might not know enough to protect herself.

Well, he couldn't do anything about it. Meanwhile, he'd use the money he'd earned working for Mr. Finelli for flowers, tickets, tuxedo rental, and everything else that a gala affair at Chrystal Mall demanded of him.

* * *

Elizabeth Chrystal stayed in her room.

It was a room worth staying in. She had recently redecorated it, having come across a color of pale peach silk she just had to have. After the tiny Empire love seat was reupholstered in peach, nothing in the rest of the room looked just right, so she did that over, too, from the walls to the drapes to the custom-made writing paper lying on the tiny cherry writing desk.

The room was large and faced south, so that sun poured in the windows. It faded the fabric, which she didn't like, but it made the room warm and golden and sunny.

And safe.

It always felt safe here.

The maid brought up her breakfast. This was rare. Mrs. Chrystal was usually out of the house very early, getting to work on her social activities. She had lunch in her room, too, but although the quiche was excellent and lay delicately on a bed of greens on her favorite china, she didn't eat it. She poked a pattern of fork holes in it and sent it back.

The maid left at one o'clock.

The house was terrifyingly empty. Every memory of every awful thing Montgomery had ever done swept back over Elizabeth Chrystal. Pulling her silken robe closely about her she tiptoed to her bedroom door and listened in fear to the creaks in her huge house.

Then she locked herself in.

Josh did not have cabin fever.

He had spring fever. Not for flowers, not for warmth. But for love. He would never have said such a thing to another person. He didn't actually form the words in his own head. But thoughts of Chelsea formed like a mist in his brain, and drifting clouds composed of her touch and her laugh and her perfume enveloped him in whatever he did. The lyrics of every rock love song he had ever heard came true and he ached for her. *A total eclipse of the heart*, he sang to himself.

He loved her name. Chelsea was strong and unusual, like the girl herself. And Chrystal was a perfect ending: fragile, beautiful, sparkling.

In English he stared at her hair. She wore it differently than other girls. Very smooth, with the barest hint of curl, it was tucked against her head. It dipped in front and was shorter in back. Sleek, golden, it slid like a whisper whenever she moved.

Josh was a confident person. Moving to Chrystal Falls had been frightening. His first weeks playing tennis had been as unsettling as anything he'd known. How was he to understand that his arrival ruined the star status of Ryan Simpson? But he had handled it.

Things settled into place. Hs mother and sister appeared to be happy. Chrystal Falls wasn't the greatest city in the world, but it wasn't the armpit of the nation either.

It had Chelsea, and that raised it considerably.

Chelsea liked him, obviously. But how much?

She had Ryan like an object on a shelf. Josh didn't want to be possessed like that. He suspected that Chelsea would run like a deer if anyone expected *her* to be an object on a shelf.

But Chelsea was an owner. She had an owner's thoughts toward everything. She tended to own her friends just as she owned her car and her jewelry. She even referred to the mall as "my mall," although he knew that the family actually owned only a small percentage of Chrystal Mall.

He shrank from that. He could not be owned by anybody, even Chelsea Chrystal. And yet he adored her.

They'd gotten together three times now. Not dates. Just things that had worked out smoothly. Now he wanted to ask her out for something special. They had to have one real date together that was unusual and terrific, before he could consider asking if she would go with him to the Chrystal Mall gala.

He'd racked his brain for two days. He wanted to make Ryan's company look boring.

Ryan liked to golf or swim or watch television.

But he'd had an idea. Two weeks ago he'd been listening to Chelsea and his sister Dawn and Perky babbling and somehow it came up that not one of them had ever flown in a small plane.

Neither had Josh. The few times he'd flown, it had been a major airline from a major airport. But of course Chrystal Falls had a small airport with small jets and planes to be chartered at any time. All he needed was money.

He wouldn't ask Chelsea to go *out* with him.

He'd ask her to go *up* with him!

Josh did not know what most people in Chrystal Falls could have told him. There was indeed a company plane, on which Mr. Chrystal and the Judge and Lillian Chrystal frequently flew. But Monty had once tried to seize the controls from the pilot and the pilot thereafter refused to take off if a youthful Chrystal was in the plane. And that was why Chelsea had never been in a small plane.

After school, when Josh was driving in secret excitement to the tiny airport to investigate his terrific idea, Chelsea came home alone to a silent house. Amy was at gymnastics practice. Her grandparents were gone, her father working.

Chelsea ran up the wide, curving stairs, her feet soundless on the thick carpet. Knocking on her mother's door, she called, "Mother? It's me, Chelsea. I want to tell you about my day."

Slowly her mother opened the door. Her hair was uncombed. Her lovely silken dressing gown was buttoned wrong. "Mother?" said Chelsea, aghast.

"Your brother telephoned."

"What did he want?" said Chelsea.

"A car." Elizabeth Chrystal's face twitched. "I told him to call your father."

"That was right, Mother." Chelsea was horrified to see her mother's fingernails were bitten. Her mother, who prized her elegant hands the way Chelsea prized her hair.

"Mother, can we go to New York this weekend? I've got to find a dress. Time is running out. I'd lost track, but the dance is coming right up."

Her mother looked confused.

"To open Chrystal Mall, Mother!" exclaimed Chelsea. "How could you forget? It's the most important thing in my life right now! And I don't have a dress. We have to go this weekend, okay?"

Her mother had a paperback book in one hand, with a finger keeping her place. It was one of those very thick family sagas, where you find out all the scandal and romance for five generations through war and peace. Chelsea detested them. She preferred books she could finish in an evening.

Elizabeth Chrystal opened the book and continued reading.

"Mother, what about New York?" Chelsea cried.

"I don't want to go anywhere just now."

"But Mother, I have to! It's our mall, and it's my opening. Everybody's always told me I'm a princess and I want to be a real one that night. I need a dress fit for a princess."

"I think you can manage with something you have," said her mother.

"No, I can't!" said Chelsea desperately. "I've never had an occasion for a dress like that, Mother. I really and truly don't have a thing to wear for this kind of event. And there's nothing in town. We have to go to New York."

Her mother turned a page in the book. Talk about escape literature, thought Chelsea. She is literally escaping from our conversation into that book. She felt like ripping the book up the spine, so her mother would look up, and acknowledge that Chelsea was standing there — with real needs and real wishes and a very real deadline.

"Mother," she began again.

"I'm afraid you'll have to make do," said her mother. "I'm not up to traveling. I know it's hard. But think of it as a lesson in life.

Perhaps if we had been harder on your brother all these years, he'd have learned a few of life's lessons, too." She turned another page in the book.

"Mother, that's not logical!" said Chelsea, almost screaming. "*I'm* the good one. Punish Monty if you want to punish someone. *I* haven't done anything. Don't deprive me of a dress because you should have been more strict with Monty."

She and her mother both loved clothes. She could not believe her mother did not understand how important this was.

"Get the dress downtown," said Elizabeth Chrystal.

"Mother," said Chelsea, struggling to be polite. "It would be such fun to get away for a few days. Your friend Lavinia would be thrilled to have us. And you could stay on! Opera and theater and museums and all those wonderful restaurants. You'd have a lovely time. You wouldn't have to worry about Monty at all."

She should not have mentioned Monty again. Her mother shivered slightly and wrapped herself even more tightly in the slightly soiled dressing gown. Chelsea had never seen her mother like this. She's having a nervous breakdown, thought Chelsea. She cannot bear another confrontation with Monty. She was not joking in Daddy's office when she said she couldn't bear it.

But I can't bear not to have a princess' dress! "Mother," she tried one more time.

"*No!*"

Chelsea spent the rest of the evening lying on her bed staring at the ceiling. No trip to New York. That meant no dress unless she bought it in town. Well, there wasn't any place in Chrystal Falls to buy anything! And what there was would be picked over by girls like — like Karen Pickett, and other mill hands' kids! It was unthinkable.

Oh, Monty Chrystal, thought his sister, weeping on her pillow, oh, how you can destroy my life without even trying!

"Mother, whatever are you doing?" exclaimed Karen Pickett. It was one o'clock in the morning, and still her mother had not gone to bed. She was at the kitchen table, sewing. "I know you adore mending, Mother, but in the middle of the night?" Karen laughed sleepily and got the glass of water she needed. Waking up a bit, she took a closer look at the fabric her mother was cutting.

"Mother! That's beautiful!" Karen touched the cloth: silken, shimmery. Vivid colors that ran into each other like molten metals. "What in the world are you making?" Karen breathed.

They were poor. The layoff was over, her father was back at work, but there was no extra cash. Fabric like this? She could not even imagine what it cost a yard.

"Remember I signed up for the bus trip that the union sponsored into Philadelphia? Everybody else went out for lunch before we went to the theater, but I wandered down to an imported fabric shop. This was on sale! See why? These nubby spots six inches from the selvage. I've been able to cut around them and still use most of the fabric."

Mrs. Pickett was an excellent seamstress. She sewed and knitted for herself and Karen, but this material was fit for a princess.

A princess.

Karen looked at her mother and Gloria Pickett looked back. Their identical eyes sparkled. Karen whispered, "For the dance? For me?"

Her mother nodded.

Karen snatched up the Vogue pattern envelope. What a dress! So elegant, and yet so in style. Perfect for a girl still in her teens. And in that fabric!

"You'll be the belle of the ball," said her mother softly. "When I heard that Chelsea Chrystal was going to New York for her dress, and probably spending hundreds of dollars plus matching shoes and her grandmother's magnificent jewels, I just couldn't stand it. I had to have something special for you."

Karen held a scrap of the cloth up to her

face and looked at herself in the hall mirror. Never had a color combination so perfectly suited her thick, dark hair, her smooth complexion, and oversized dark eyes.

I will be the beautiful one, thought Karen.

I, the mill hand's daughter. It will be just like Cinderella. No matter what Chelsea wears, she'll just be a thin, showy blonde. *I will be the beautiful one.*

"Are you pleased with it, honey?" said Gloria Pickett anxiously.

"Oh, Mother, I love it."

Karen even took a scrap of fabric back to bed with her, twining the silk over and around her fingers. She slept like a child with a secret under her pillow.

Chapter
Seven

Quivering with excitement, Dawn left high
school for her first afternoon tutoring Gideon.
She didn't even pause to find Pete, and talk
with him for a few minutes. He didn't like
this tutoring idea, and she didn't want him
to dampen her spirits.

She didn't admit to herself that she was
also a little excited about meeting Monty
again. There was something about Monty that
drew her closer. A moth to the flame? she
thought.

She drove in the rutted lane, bouncing uncomfortably into the backyard of Halfway
House. How lovely it was back here! There
were enough evergreens and enough shelter to
keep it pretty even at the end of winter. She
could just imagine how lovely it would be
when the daffodil bed burst into gaudy yellow

and the immense knotted forsythia bushes colored the whole west side of the lawn.

Gideon was waiting for her. He did not look happy.

"How was school today?" said Dawn brightly.

He shrugged. "You know. School."

Dawn loved school. Not so much the classes, as the friends and the action and the company. She felt sorry for anybody who had to spend all those years there and didn't like it. "What are your favorite courses?" she asked next.

Gideon looked at her as if she were crazy. How could he possibly have favorite courses? Nothing in school was worth more than a shrug and a lot of it was just plain rotten.

Dawn and Gideon sat in the glassed-in porch, surrounded by thriving plants, but the plants were the only successful ones there. Gideon gave Dawn no help at all. Even when she got out her magazines, he just looked at her.

Dawn was close to tears.

What a slap in the face, she thought. Here I was going to save the world and I can't even get Gideon to talk to me, let alone start learning how to read.

Screaming sirens from the highway interrupted them. Dawn waited until the noise was over. To her surprise, Gideon leaped up, racing to the window, hoping to catch a glimpse of the fire engines. "Too many bushes and trees around here," said Gideon darkly. "You can't see anything."

"You like fire engines?" said Dawn.

"I love 'em. That's what I want to be. A fireman."

There — she had found it. The wedge that would start Gideon's interest. They talked about fire fighters, about trucks and hoses and life-saving equipment. Dawn said, "My brother Josh read a terrific book about being a fire fighter in New York City. I'll get that from the library and we'll start reading it."

Gideon stopped talking instantly. The thought of reading a whole book obviously upset him. But Dawn was sure of herself now. She said, "Look. In the back of this electronics magazine are all kinds of ads for plectrons — the kind that pick up all the local emergency wave lengths, so you can listen in on the ambulance and fire and police calls. Let's read those."

Gideon lit up again. Reading an ad three lines long didn't scare him. And a plectron was something he would love to have. Together he and Dawn stumbled through an entire column of ads — and it was Dawn who gave up first. *Her* interest in plectrons was extremely limited! She didn't know how to teach reading, but she did know one thing — Gideon had already memorized the words he needed to read this particular kind of thing.

It's not saving the world, she thought wryly,

but it's a bigger vocabulary for Gideon and I guess I'll have to settle for that.

They filled the next hour playing Monopoly, because you had to read all the chance and community chest cards. Gideon was pretty good.

"Hey," said a deep male voice, "how come you didn't tell me it was all fun and games out here? I would have played, too."

She turned to see Monty Chrystal.

Dawn usually smiled instinctively at anyone who greeted her, but this time the smile didn't reach her lips easily. Monty was staring at her — a scorching, intense look she could not understand. It made her curiously breathless, and instead of smiling she licked her lips and said very awkwardly, "Well, it wasn't a very exciting game."

"I would have made it exciting," said Monty, in that strange graveled voice that rasped over her nerves today as it had done before.

He sat down next to her. Very close. Then he hitched his chair even closer. Dawn swallowed. Monty began to deal himself some money so he could begin playing.

Gideon said quickly, "Here, you just play me, Monty. I'm doing pretty well. You'll already own Boardwalk and Park Place and I've got houses on Baltic Avenue."

Monty never looked at Gideon. Nodding slowly, he swiveled the entire round table, so that Gideon's money and cards were now in front of him, but Dawn was still next to him. The dice lay in Dawn's palm. Monty uncurled her fingers and took the dice right out of her hand.

His hand was enormous. Not a ham hock, not a workman's hand; there were no callouses. His was a very large variation of Chelsea's — long fingers, wide palm, and strong. Dawn found herself wanting to hold that hand, seize back her dice, and make him try for them again.

How big Monty was compared to Gideon! Gideon was just a scrawny little adolescent. Monty was a man.

How could he stand it — being cooped up with a bunch of children? Why didn't he just demand from his parents the money and the job that must be his by right?

Monty juggled the dice in his hand. Dawn looked into his eyes. What strange calculating expressions he wore! If only she knew what he meant by them. She uncurled his fingers right back, and drew the dice between her fingers. She said, "No fair rushing your turn, Monty."

Monty said, "I never bother with being fair."

Dawn giggled at this teasing. It did not occur to her this was a statement of fact.

Monty snapped his fingers in Gideon's direction. "Get us something to drink, kid."

103

Gideon was gone like a shadow, and returned in record time with two Cokes poured over ice.

"You've started your own training program?" said Dawn to Monty. She took her turn. It was obvious that she was going to land on a railroad — the only one she didn't yet own. Monty took a die, turned it over so she now had a different number and said, "Too bad. You missed the railroad."

Dawn, laughing, said, "How will we ever finish the game if you change all the rules?" But she accepted the change, and landed on one of his properties instead, and paid him the rent he demanded.

Monty grinned. Now Dawn could see the resemblance to Chelsea again: that expression that simply *expected* you to fall in line. I am a Chrystal. If I say it's all right, then it's all right.

The Chrystals had a sense of power that few could argue with. In Chelsea it resulted in jealousy from some, following from others, and admiration (reluctant or not) from almost all. Dawn was not sure what kind of power Monty had. But it was there. It tantalized her. She laughed as he arranged the entire game so that he would win. Gideon, standing back from them, the magazine with the radio ads folded open in his hand, did not laugh.

At five o'clock, when Monty had most of the property and all of the money, Dawn conceded. She got up, saying her mother expected her home. "That was fun," she said, trying to include both Gideon and Monty in her smile. But the smile stuck on Monty and never traveled to Gideon. Something in Monty caught her, as if he had barbs to trap her by. As she stood up, so did he, and he loomed over her, far broader and taller than anybody she had ever dated.

He made his right hand into a fist and set it under her chin and raised the chin an inch so that she was staring up into his eyes. The size of the fist, the bunching of the arm muscles, terrified her. For a frightened moment, she wanted to run. Monty laughed, deep in his throat, and Dawn thought, he wanted to scare me! He did that to be funny.

Now in his eyes was a wide amusement, and she laughed at herself, and laughed with Monty, and she had a very unexpected desire. To fling herself upon that broad chest and demand kisses, as he had demanded victory in the board game.

Confused, startled, Dawn turned away from him. She thought, It's Pete I love. What's with this funny feeling toward Monty? She could not stop herself from glancing back as she walked to her car. Monty was looking at her with a mocking triumph in his eyes. She flushed scarlet and practically ducked into her car. He knows, thought Dawn. He knows I wanted to kiss him.

* * *

At the Chrystal household, all serenity was gone.

"What do you mean, you're going to the Far East for a month?" cried Chelsea.

"We've been wanting to go to Japan and Hong Kong for a long, long time," explained her grandmother. "My old college roommate has moved to Hawaii. We talked on the phone the other day and it seemed the ideal time for a visit. We'll spend a week with her and then fly on to the Orient."

"The ideal time?" repeated Chelsea. Her mother was closeted in her bedroom, collapsing under the strain of Monty's return; her brother Monty was on the phone to them at all hours demanding money, release, a car, anything. And this was the ideal time to go abroad?

"How did you make arrangements so fast?" said Amy, who thought it was exciting.

"When your grandmother decides on something, it's as good as done," said Judge Chrystal, smiling. "We're flying out tomorrow afternoon. I can hardly wait. I feel like a kid. I feel about forty."

Amy laughed hysterically at the idea of forty being a kid. She said, "I want to come, too. Can't you bring me along? I'm only in seventh grade. Nothing that matters."

They patted Amy indulgently and didn't bother to answer.

Alexander Chrystal turned to Chelsea. "Well, my dear," he said to his older daughter, smiling, "I believe running the household will be in your hands now. I have so much work to do I'm going to be eating meals right at the office and I just won't be around. We'll be counting on you, Chelsea."

"Oh, good," said Amy. "Now we can order pizza every night."

Chelsea tried to smile, but it was impossible. Did they understand what they were doing? They were running away. They were doing exactly what Chelsea's mother had done! Elizabeth Chrystal was hiding in her room; Grandmother and Grandfather Chrystal were fleeing across the Pacific Ocean; Alexander Chrystal was going to immerse himself in his work, and since he had a secretary to answer the phone, he could screen himself entirely from Monty.

Chelsea sat alone at the abandoned dinner table.

Her grandparents were in a flurry of packing; Amy was mucking out the stables; her father had kept to his word and gone back to the office; her mother had sent her tray back down, the food uneaten. The maid asked for a week off to visit her children in Florida and Chelsea weakly agreed that this would be a good time. The cook thought it would be nice to fix a lot of meals and freeze them and she herself would visit her sister in Jamaica.

Chelsea nodded helplessly.

How can this be happening? she thought. They're deserting me. I don't want to be captain of this ship! I don't want to have anything to do with this house or with Monty!

Of course, that evening the telephone rang ceaselessly. Her mother had taken out the phone in her own room by the simple expedient of unplugging the jack. Chelsea answered all the calls, hoping for Josh.

But no — it was the bridge tournament organizer, wanting to know if they could still meet next Tuesday at the Chrystal mansion. Chelsea told them she thought they'd better shift to the club.

And then it was the flower committee at church — her mother had signed up last year to be responsible for the Sunday flowers. Chelsea pressed her forehead. "Yes, of course," she said. She made a note to herself to call the florist in the morning to handle that one.

Just before she left, the maid popped her head in to say that a few more slate tiles had come off the roof and Miss Chelsea should probably get someone to repair that before the roof started leaking. "Who does that work?" said Chelsea.

"I have no idea," said the maid. "Ask your mother."

Amy wanted to know could Maggie spend

tomorrow night even if it was a school night, and Chelsea said no and had a rousing fight with her sister and the phone rang again.

She almost didn't answer it.

With the way her luck was running, it was probably Monty.

"Hello," she said wearily, on the ninth ring.

"Miss Chelsea Chrystal, please." It was a very authoritative voice. At least it wasn't Monty.

"This is she," sighed Chelsea, wishing she could pretend it wasn't.

"Miss Chrystal, I am the scheduling director for the eleven o'clock news at the Philadelphia television station. We've received the publicity releases about the gala opening of the new Chrystal Mall. Your photograph is in the flyer as the one to cut the ribbon and start the dancing."

"Why, yes," she said, startled.

"We want to send a crew to cover the occasion, of course. We just wanted you to know that we'll be interviewing you, and you'll be on the eleven o'clock news, probably a three minute segment, and in the morning they'll probably pick up a one minute spot as well."

I'll be on television! thought Chelsea.

Her anxieties vanished in a heartbeat. Excited and thrilled, she questioned the scheduling director, getting details, thinking, I, I, Chelsea Chrystal, will not only be the star of the ball — I'll be the star on television!

Joy restored, Chelsea hung up and hugged herself. Handling silly things like florists and roofers seemed well within her powers now.

She let herself slide into a wonderful daydream. In her dream, an important producer doing a new, sophisticated evening soap opera like *Dallas* would be in Philadelphia watching the news. Just as he was yawning and thinking of falling asleep, he would see Chelsea in her lovely gown and he'd sit up straight, eyes bright, because he'd found the girl he was looking for! Elegant, aristocratic, stunningly beautiful, she would be perfect for the new part. She would get another phone call in the morning, and they'd beg her to —

But she did not have any gown at all, let alone a lovely one. Chelsea leaped to her feet, galvanized by the horror of being dressless on such an occasion. Racing up the stairs she banged on her mother's bedroom door. "Guess what!" she cried breathlessly, hugging her mother. "We're going to be on television! The night of the ball!"

But her mother shrank back. "Television?" she repeated, as if it frightened her. "I don't believe I'll be going anyway. It doesn't matter."

Her mother! The finest, most graceful hostess in the city, afraid to appear at her own spectacular occasion?

Chelsea felt a stab of actual fear. "Mama,"

she said, a name she had not used for her mother in years, "Mama, it'll be fine. Really. All we need to do is go to New York and — "

Her mother gently tugged her toward the door. "I don't know why you keep running on about New York, Chelsea. I simply can't undertake anything when I feel so under the weather. Really, you are old enough now to handle your own problems. Television! Ugh. Now run on to bed, dear, please. Run on to bed, please. Run on to. . . ." Her mother's voice faded like a run-down toy.

Chelesa backed out of the room.

What am I going to do? she thought.

Television now seemed not a thrill but a disaster. Was it going to immortalize her in some frumpy reject of a dress — wrong hemline, wrong cut, wrong fabric, wrong color?

If only I had somebody on my team! she thought, fighting the tears that threatened to envelop her. She could not give in to crying. Locking yourself in your room was what happened when you surrendered to tears.

But I do have somebody on my team, she thought. I have Josh.

Chelsea ran to the privacy of her own room and dialed the Newhouse number.

At Halfway House Monty Chrystal seethed with rage. The Sheffields were refusing him everything. He couldn't leave the premises. He had to do stupid, worthless, physical chores. He was actually supposed to split wood for the fire, and paint the shed in the back and clean all the attic windows so they could put another bedroom up there for yet another boy.

Boy, thought Monty Chrystal grimly, I'm stuck in here with all these little boys. Stupid, worthless, empty-headed little fourteen-year-olds with pimples and buck teeth.

Chrystal Falls had very little action — unless, of course, he started some — but at least something happened out there! Now he was stuck here in this dark house with these straight-laced, worthless house parents. When he called his father he got the secretary. When he called the house he got the maid or Chelsea.

They can't do this to me, thought Montgomery Chrystal. I'm not hanging around here. I'm leaving. I'm going where the action is.

And to do that, he needed money. A lot of it. Monty dismissed the thought of stealing it. He wanted a lot more than he was apt to find in a random theft, and anyway, he didn't want to risk being caught. They were leaving old Chels in charge of the house now, and that meant she had access to money.

It made him sick.

Chelsea — arrogant, snobby, skinny sister of his — getting the family money when he wasn't even allowed an allowance by Halfway House rules.

Well, he would get money out of Chelsea. He didn't care what he had to resort to. There was a way to snap her. There was a way to snap anybody's bones if you tried hard enough.

"Josh," said Chelsea Chrystal into the phone, "I need you."

If there was any finer sentence in the English language, Josh did not know it. To be needed by the girl he loved! It was like words from heaven.

Of course, when Chelsea needed him, Dawn had the car.

Cruel fate slaps me down again, thought Josh, trying to make himself laugh. Desperately hating being a knight in shining armor who couldn't even drive up to the door, let alone perform the rescue, Josh said, "I don't have a car, Chels. Otherwise I'd be there at a hundred miles an hour."

"I'll drive to you," she said. "It's late. Can you still go out?"

"Sure," said Josh, and he slipped out of the house to meet her.

Monty laughed.

He shared a bedroom with Gideon, who was afraid of him. The laugh woke Gideon out of a deep sleep, and Gideon lay motionless between the sheets and blankets, trying to regulate his breathing. He did not like the sound of that laugh. He did not want Monty to explain what was so funny. Monty had a very sick sense of humor.

Monty was, in fact, a very sick person.

Gideon wondered about the strange girl, Dawn. How could a nice, sweet girl like that enjoy Monty's company? Perhaps she just couldn't see what Monty was. Well, he, Gideon, would not tell her. It was too dangerous. Monty would kill him.

Josh opened the passenger door of Chelsea's convertible, slid onto the leather seat all the way next to her, and kissed her. She opened her arms and they hugged and kissed for the first time, urgently, intently. Josh kissed her with adoration, but she kissed him with desperation, and he could feel it.

He was the first to break away.

She didn't allow it, but leaned back into his arms and made him hold her.

"What's wrong?" he said. He felt wonderful. No matter what was wrong with her life, everything was right with his. He felt powerful. He, Josh Newhouse, could make it all better for Chelsea Chrystal.

She burst into tears.

"I'll drive," said Josh, getting out and walking around the car. He put the car in drive and Chelsea snuggled up against him and he wrapped one arm around her. Very slowly, he eased the car away from the apartment buildings. It was a very cold night, but the car was certainly going to keep them comfortable. He headed for a dead-end road that overlooked Chrystal Falls. There had been a bridge there once, right below the falls, but a great hurricane fifty years earlier had wiped the span out. Now there was a wonderful place to view the splashing, violent waters, and the night lights from the factories lit the water.

They parked by the edge of the cliff, staring down into the raging white water.

"My life is like that right now," said Chelsea.

"Tell me," said Josh, and they sat very close, tangled in each other, and Chelsea started to tell him about Monty. She was being honest with Josh, because she loved him, and in her honesty the real truth poured out. Monty was not upsetting her a fraction as much as the lack of a dress was.

"It's so stupid," she said at first. "You wouldn't understand."

"Sure I would. I have a sister and a mother, don't I? Lots of feminine experience."

Chelsea made a face. "I have a father and a brother, and I can tell you they haven't learned a thing about women just because there are three of us around."

Josh grinned. "I didn't claim I learned anything, Chels. Just struggled to understand."

She touched his hand, and it obeyed her and touched back the way she needed to be touched. "Okay," she said. "Confession. Here it comes. If you laugh. . . ."

"I won't," he promised.

She decided to risk it. "You know how everyone calls me The Princess? And they're not very nice about it?"

Josh nodded.

Chelsea looked at him intensely in the dim light. "I really *want* to be a princess," she said. "I think about this dance coming up at the mall and I want to come down a crystal staircase in glass slippers. I want to be so lovely that every other girl will fade into the background. Oh, Josh, it's terrible. It's so egotistical. I mean, here's your sister Dawn wanting to volunteer herself to save the world and all I care about is having the nicest dress. But I *love* the idea of being a princess. *It's what I want.*"

Josh did not laugh. His face seemed to harden in the darkness. She could see its lines and hollows far more clearly. "But I do understand," he told her. "I want to be King."

She thought he meant Prince Charming. Her prince, at the royal ball.

But he said, "King of the Courts. Crown Prince of tennis. Oh, Chelsea, I want to win on every court in the world. I want to beat the competition from England and Norway and Australia and Brazil. I want to be the finest men's tennis player in the world. I want my picture on the cover of *Sports Illustrated* and my house filled with my trophies."

They could hardly believe what each had said. Neither Chelsea nor Josh had ever said those dreams out loud, and to find them shared by the first person they confessed to — it kept them silent.

Chelsea said, "I shouldn't care so much."

Josh shook his head. "People who say they don't care are lying. Of course they care. Nobody wants to be dull or a loser. It's just that you and I are willing to admit what we want. I want to be number one in tennis. You want to be a princess."

They both laughed a little and kissed again.

"Seems reasonable enough to me," said Chelsea. "The king and the princess. We're naturals, Josh." Her voice was so soft he could hardly hear it. Her lips brushed across his skin and his arms tightened around her.

She did not mention her brother. Why spoil a perfect moment? And so the only one of Chelsea's troubles that Josh knew of was the lack of a dress. And they got so involved talking about themselves as king and princess they didn't even remember to solve that one.

Monty escaped attention for the reason he always did: It was too painful to think of him. It was easier to pretend he wasn't there.

Chapter Eight

The following day in school was a flurry of activity. The entire school seemed to be rushing from one frantic activity to another, without a moment to exchange gossip or relax in the student lounge. Perky Palmer had gone into Philadelphia for her dress, which she described at length to a captive audience in gym. Karen Pickett listened silently, and smiled a superior smile, which Perky didn't miss. How could Karen feel superior to me? thought Perky. She thought smugly of the amount of money her mother had spent on dress, shoes, earrings, and special bra and slip. No mill hand's daughter could spend a fraction of that. If Karen Pickett was smiling, it was acting.

Chelsea shrugged when asked about her dress.

Perky didn't know if this was acting or not. It wasn't like Chelsea not to give out details. But it was unthinkable that she actually *didn't know* what she was wearing, with barely two weeks left till the ball.

Everyone was calling it a ball now, with giggles; and anyone who didn't have a dress yet was called Cinderella. "Your fairy godmother going to wave her wand over you at the last minute?" teased one of Perky's friends when another girl admitted she hadn't started looking yet. "There's nothing left in Chrystal Falls, that's for sure. And Perky picked over everything in Philadelphia. Nothing there."

"It's a rather large city," observed Karen. "I feel sure Perky didn't pass by every single available dress."

Perky smiled viciously. "No, I didn't," she agreed. "There are a lot of cheap stores you can still visit, Karen."

"Girls, girls," said Dawn. Dawn was in a bright, happy mood that nothing could interfere with, and she wasn't going to let fussing between the Hill and Mill factions get started.

"What's your dress like?" Karen asked her.

"Where'd you buy it?" added Perky.

Dawn just laughed. "I went to a really spectacular affair just a month before we moved to Chrystal Falls and I've only worn the dress once and none of you have seen it. It's absolutely perfect. I'm going to be the best-dressed woman on the dance floor."

She said this with such assurance that both Perky and Karen were a little thrown.

Chelsea felt like ripping her hair out. Every girl expected to be the best-dressed one there.

"What color is yours going to be?" Dawn asked Chelsea.

What will they do to me if I lie down in the hall and start screaming at the top of my lungs? thought Chelsea Chrystal. Will they lock me up? That sounds pretty restful, actually. My family can afford the very finest in mental institutions. I'll get art therapy, golf therapy, music therapy, swimming pool therapy. She said with a smile, "Secrets, secrets. You'll have to wait for the big night. By the way, I'll be on television. Philadelphia news is sending a crew to cover the event."

That distracted them! Chelsea slipped her arm through Dawn's, ignoring Perky's look of jealousy, and walked down the hall. "Where is Josh?" she said. "I can't seem to find him."

"In the gym, I think," said Dawn. "He got a chance to go to some big regional tennis championship he didn't think he qualified for. Some indoor thing in New York someplace. He's filling out the papers."

Chelsea made herself walk to the gym. Maybe the championship involved a few hours' drive each direction. Maybe it wasn't a big thing. After all, Josh couldn't go missing school, could he? Not now when she needed him!

Josh was running out of the coach's office just as she walked down that corridor. "Chelsea!" he yelled, and he rushed to her, hugging her, swinging her around. Several people stopped to look. They were a lovely pair — dark, strong Josh; slender, golden Chelsea. For the sake of the observers she laughed and kissed him. Inside she felt like stone.

"Guess what!" he said, and went on without giving her a chance to guess. "We just found out that I can go up to the regional championships. It's a long drive and the principal wasn't going to give permission for me to miss classes for two days, but he gave in when my mother called him. We're leaving tomorrow; I'll miss Thursday and Friday, and stay through the weekend."

"And," said Chelsea, "win the title, I am absolutely sure."

"Count on it," said Josh and he kissed her again. But she thought that was the future trophy he was really hugging, and it was the game he was really thinking of, not her.

She said, "I'm going to be so proud of you, Josh."

He laughed happily. "I was afraid you'd be mad at me," he confided. "I mean, after last night — I wanted to take you out for a fantastic date this weekend."

And I wanted to go, thought Chelsea. I needed to go.

"But I knew you'd understand," said Josh,

hugging her so hard she thought he might crack a rib. She kept on smiling at him. He said, "After all, if I'm going to be a world champion, I'd better be a regional champion first, right?"

"Right!"

They sealed it with a kiss, and then another. "Got to run home and pack," said Josh, and this time the kiss meant good-bye. "Listen, I'll call you."

"Okay."

He paused and looked at her searchingly. Chelsea composed her face. He saw nothing. He said, "You can find a dress. I know you're going to look perfect. And we'll have the first dance, right?"

"The second. First is with my father."

"Second dance, here I come," said Josh. But he was already off down the hall, thinking of first place and blue ribbons. Chelsea was forgotten.

Never in her entire life had she felt so totally alone.

She did not cry. She did not permit herself to contemplate crying. It was important to carry this off. She would go home and think calmly and handle this dress thing by herself.

Ryan Simpson saw them part and he was eaten up by jealousy.

Chelsea could do no wrong in his eyes. It was Josh Newhouse who started things, roiled up serene waters, ruined his, Ryan's, life.

Ryan took refuge in his usual tactic, which was to drive away from the problem too fast.

Pete and Mitch were already working at the mall. They were driving one of the dump trucks on a dump run. The back was filled with debris — torn sheetrock, broken tile, empty electrical fixture boxes, packing crates, a million soda cans. They loved the dump run. Twelve miles of driving a powerful truck. They and the truck were so dusty as to be anonymous.

And certainly Ryan Simpson, when he passed them in a no passing zone at much too high a rate of speed, never knew who was driving the dump truck.

"If I felt like it," said Pete, who was driving, "I could drive right over his little sports car. Squash him like a bug on the sidewalk."

"Tempting," nodded Mitch, and they grinned at each other.

"Or park next to him," said Pete, dreamily, "and accidentally dump this load of garbage on him."

They drove on, however, content to threaten Ryan without doing anything about him. He wasn't worth it.

Chelsea got home without crying out loud, and at home she continued to stay calm because Amy mustn't see how tense Chelsea was.

Her father telephoned to say he was eating at the club. Chelsea didn't feel up to the facile chatter she would have to make if she and Amy joined him. Anyway, if she told her father about the dress, he would never understand. Clothing was her mother's realm. Daddy thought clothing just appeared naturally in the closet. His secretary paid the bills; he didn't even bother with that aspect. He wouldn't see how important it was — how there was only one weekend left — how this whole thing could be a complete, humiliating disaster.

As for Amy, she'd been out horseback riding all afternoon and was grubby. She didn't want to shower and change and go to the club. She didn't even want to clean up enough to eat in the dining room. So Chelsea heated one of the frozen meals the cook had prepared, and Amy took a tray upstairs to their mother.

The girls ate in the kitchen. Chelsea hated it. Very old-fashioned, it had three rooms: a back pantry for cold things and vegetables; a central kitchen with appliances and sink; and a butler's pantry for china, silver, and crystal. Never modernized, it probably never would be. None of the Chrystals cooked and it didn't matter much if the staff found it inefficient. So the old white tiles, the big porcelain sink on feet, and the awkwardly placed old kitchen table stayed.

Amy thought the room had character.

Chelsea thought it was repulsive and dank.

When the phone rang, Amy tilted back in her chair to reach the wall phone behind her. The chair slipped on the ceramic floor and Amy fell with a crash. Both girls screamed, the phone fell on the floor, and the receiver was chipped. Amy, lying unhurt on the floor, said "Hello?" as if nothing had happened.

Nobody would believe I live like this, thought Chelsea. She hoped it was Josh, calling to tell her he wasn't going. Calling to say he knew she must have more problems than just a dress and could he come over and listen to her talk about them. Calling to say he loved her so passionately he couldn't be away even for a tennis tournament.

Uh huh, thought Chelsea. Spin me another.

Into the phone Amy was saying things like, "Yeah. Umm. Well. Huh. Mmmm."

"Who's that?" said Chelsea.

"It's Monty. He's so lucky he lives at Halfway House. He always has company. I wish I could go away to school. How come he's always the lucky one?"

Chelsea thought, I could just brain her with the phone. It would be hard on the phone, but it might knock some sense in her. "He's been on a good luck streak all his life," Chelsea told her sister grimly.

"He wants to talk to you," said Amy, tossing the phone at Chelsea. "Can I eat my supper in the TV room?"

Chelsea missed the phone. It landed in the butter.

Chelsea wrapped the buttered phone with her napkin. "You can eat your supper in the sewage treatment plant for all I care," she said.

Amy glared at her. "Don't yell at *me* just because you haven't got a dumb dress," said Amy. "Show a little spunk. Go to New York by yourself and get it instead of hanging around whining." Amy picked up her plate and fork, balanced her glass on the crook of her arm, and left the room.

"Yes?" said Chelsea to her brother.

"It's me."

"I know."

There was silence. Chelsea considered hanging up on Monty. She knew what he was going to say. He'd demand money and make threats. She should stop the conversation before it started.

But he would just call back.

Monty said, "Let me talk to our dear mother."

"No," said Chelsea. A good thing her mother's phone wasn't connected. If Elizabeth Chrystal had to talk to Monty right now, she would collapse completely. It was funny how Monty never affected Amy. Amy had the character of a slab of granite. Nothing could damage her. We should just turn the whole family over to Amy to control, thought Chelsea. She can handle anything. She has the answers to anything.

Imagine telling me to go to New York by myself.

"There's no reason for you to talk to Mother," said Chelsea.

"Does this mean *you* are in charge?" said Monty.

"I'm not giving you a thing, Montgomery Chrystal."

Monty swore viciously into her ear. "You have everything, girl. Money. Status. Good grades. Friends. Social position. Boyfriend. Clothes. Car. And a tankful of gas."

"I deserve them," said Chelsea.

"Oh, right. You have all that because you're so wonderful. You don't deserve one thing, sister mine."

"Well, I deserve it more than you," she retorted. "You've never earned anything in your life."

"Are you pretending that *you* earned something?" said Monty, furious. "It isn't *your* money, Chelsea. It's your ancestors' money. You've never earned a dime in your life. I'm the oldest, anyhow, and if it's anybody's money, it's mine."

"Forget it," said Chelsea. This isn't so bad, she thought. I just keep saying forget it until he gives up and gets off the phone.

He said, "I could trash that beautiful new mall of yours."

"You couldn't. They have guards and attack dogs there, Monty. I know because Pete Carter and Mitch Boyd are working there and they said after one of the dirt loaders, worth seventy-five thousand dollars, was stolen, they really tightened security. So even if you could get away from Halfway House you couldn't touch Chrystal Mall."

"What do you mean — *if* I could get away?" demanded Monty. "This isn't a jail. It's a house with house parents. I can walk out any time I feel like it. The thing is, Chelsea, I don't feel like walking. I feel like driving. And for that I need a car and I need money."

"They won't let you," said Chelsea irritably.

"Since when have I cared whether or not they *let* me?" said Monty.

Chelsea remained silent, waiting for him to give up. His threats weren't much, after all. She wouldn't put her mother on the phone and she wouldn't give in to his demands for money and that was that.

"I'm leaving Chrystal Falls for good," said Monty, "and you have to give me the money."

"Much as I want you to leave for good," Chelsea said, "I will not pay the tab. You behave yourself, you get a job, you earn your own money, and then you leave."

Monty called her another assortment of names. If their mother had listened in on this conversation she would have had cardiac arrest. Chelsea just waited for it to end. She wiped the butter off the receiver. "You don't have a job or earn your own way," Monty pointed out. "Now get me some cash."

"I don't have any money," said Chelsea irritably. "Daddy's secretary pays the bills and you know it."

"You have your clothing allowance and your credit cards and your own bank account."

"If you had behaved yourself you'd have the same thing." Chelsea was beginning to feel very successful. Perhaps she had what it took to handle jerks like this, after all. There was a long pause. Monty was thinking up new threats. Chelsea was faintly enjoying her power.

"Cute little friend you have," said Monty at last.

"Who?" she said sharply, thinking, How could he know about Josh.

"Little Sunrise. Little Miss Happy Dawn."

The butter had soaked through her napkin onto her palm. It was a slimy feeling. Like the conversation.

"You want your little innocent friend Dawn to stay innocent?" said Monty. His voice was horrid. Low, probably because he was afraid the Sheffields would overhear. Gravelly, because that was natural to him. And dark, because he was a dark, angry man.

Chelsea swallowed. Her throat had thickened with fear. "I'll call Dad," she said, her voice breaking.

"No, Chels, you won't. This is between you and me. You call Dad and I'll drop by the house and put our mother over the edge. Easy enough to do. I have lots of experience with Mom."

He did have. And Chelsea knew how close to the breaking point her mother actually was. She could not think of one word to say to this horrible person who was her own older brother.

Gently, with a convulsive shudder, Chelsea set the phone down.

Dawn. He was threatening Dawn.

Amy came bounding into the room. "There's double chocolate cake," she said happily. "I helped ice it. It's a masterpiece, Chels. Wait till you taste it." She lifted the glass lid from the cake stand and brought in two lovely, fragile, china dessert plates and two old, silver dessert forks that had been in the Chrystal family for a hundred years.

A hundred years, thought Chelsea Chrystal grimly, and what did we end up with? Montgomery Chrystal.

"I don't want any cake, thanks," she said to her sister.

Amy shrugged and went back to her television, taking both the fat slices she had cut.

Chelsea started to go to her bedroom and found her knees actually weak. She sank back onto the wooden kitchen chair. What do I do? she thought. I can't let him hurt Dawn.

If she told her mother, her mother would collapse. She could not tell her grandfather because he had already left for Hawaii and Japan. She could go to the club now and catch her father. Or she could call the Sheffields and tell them what Monty was planning.

Her father, so decisive in all other things, would instantly call Perky's father, George Palmer, his partner. And so the long, gossipy chain would begin, as Perky and her mother took advantage of the opportunity to be the first with a juicy story.

And the Sheffields? Monty hadn't actually done anything wrong yet. All they could do was keep a closer eye on him in case he did.

Or she could telephone Dawn. Explain to Dawn that her brother was a snake.

I can't bear that, thought Chelsea. I have too much family pride. I cannot look a newcomer in the eye, one who is becoming a close friend, and whose brother I adore, and say to her, *My brother is a rotten, dangerous criminal.*

Such a person would never appear in the Newhouse family. They were all such good, decent, caring people!

I can't bear to have them think so little of us, thought Chelsea. There *must* be a way to get out from under Monty without telling anyone, without making anything worse.

Chapter Nine

Right after school, Chelsea drove to Halfway House. She might be making a tactical error, but she also might be in a position to rescue things. She would face Monty down. He was something of a bully, and in the presence of stronger people, often buckled.

It would be a test. How strong was Chelsea Chrystal?

But things got off to a bad start the moment she stopped the car behind Halfway House. Monty was sitting on the sagging back steps next to Dawn. The steps were wide enough for Monty and Dawn to sit far apart. But they weren't. They were sitting close together.

Not actually touching.

But close — very close.

Oh, no! thought Chelsea. She cannot be falling for Monty. Bad enough her taste runs to a roughneck like Pete Carter. But to enjoy my brother?

Chelsea stepped out of her car. How improbable that fine car looked sitting in those ruts, next to the unkempt garden and the rotting shed. Slim as a pencil, elegant as a model, she approached them. Her brother looked surprised and pleased. Dawn obviously thought this was a sign of affection between Monty and Chelsea and it made her happy. Chelsea knew better. It was a dollar sign — Monty figured Chelsea had given up the fight and brought him money.

"Ah," said Monty, however, always sarcastic. "The royal carriage hath arrived."

Dawn smiled at the joke, not sensing the strong antagonism that prompted it. Dawn looked up at Monty to share the amusement with him. How overwhelming his presence was! She had a feeling that most of Monty's personality was beneath the surface. If only she could draw it out, the way she was drawing from Gideon the ability to read.

"Hi, Dawn," said Chelsea. "How's the tutoring going?"

There was no sign of Gideon. In fact Monty had sent the boy on an errand. Gideon was no fool. He knew he was expected to take his time.

When Chelsea examined Dawn, her heart sank. Dawn was having a good time sitting there next to Monty. Of course, Monty had all the Chrystal charm, when he chose to use it. He was crafty; he could see through Dawn, and use her. It made him the more dangerous, and it made Chelsea's job harder, because she was not naturally a schemer.

Monty yelled into the house, "Hey! Mrs. Sheffield! Can I go for a short ride with my sister?"

Chelsea shrank from the idea.

Dawn thought it was terrible that a young man like Monty had to beg permission to spend a little while with his own sister.

Mrs. Sheffield emerged from the kitchen. Chelsea liked her looks immediately. Friendly, motherly, but tough. "I'm afraid not, Monty," said Mrs. Sheffield pleasantly. "You are limited to the grounds for another week and you have not yet finished today's chores. Dawn, dear, I think you came to tutor Gideon, did you not? Perhaps you can continue in the living room."

Dawn jumped up guiltily and ran in to tutor Gideon.

Monty shook his head, finding such attention to duty both amusing and stupid.

Chelsea thought, All right! Mrs. Sheffield can control things. Maybe I should tell her what Monty's threatening.

But Chelsea knew exactly how Mrs. Sheffield would deal with it. She would make Monty's situation tougher yet — which would infuriate Monty more, and make it more likely that Monty would take things out on their mother. And then Mrs. Sheffield would tell Dawn not to return. Fine idea. Except that Dawn would want an explanation and Chelsea desperately did not want her to have one.

She had thought she was above other people's opinions, but she was not. She wanted Dawn to think highly of the Chrystals. Especially since she was in love with Dawn's brother.

"We can just sit in the car, then," suggested Chelsea, "so we can talk privately."

Mrs. Sheffield said that would be fine, and Monty jumped up with unaccustomed alacrity to get in the passenger seat. Chelsea followed nervously. Comfortable as those leather, contoured seats were, she felt as if she was sitting on spikes. She could not bear to look in Monty's greedy, demanding eyes.

"Give me the money," said Monty instantly. "How much did you bring?"

She swallowed. "None."

"Don't play games, Chels," he said in a dangerous voice.

"I didn't bring money and I'm not going to. You don't have a threat that will make me."

There was a long silence. She watched the back door for Mrs. Sheffield.

In a vicious, grating whisper Monty called her every vile name he knew. He knew them all. Chelsea schooled herself not to flinch, no matter how bad it got. It was important to make Monty think she was shrugging it off.

"Get money," hissed her brother. "Get into your trust fund. Lie to Dad. I don't care what you do, but bring me the money. I'm getting out of Chrystal Falls and you're paying the freight. Got it, Chels?"

"You're the one who hasn't got it," she said. "For once you're not going to —"

His hand closed around her wrist and tightened. The pulse in his wrist pounded. Visible veins on the back of his hand throbbed beneath the mottled skin. She could literally feel his rage.

Chelsea tried to pull her hand back. His fingers closed painfully to prevent it.

She looked at him, keeping her face clear of fear. Her brother leaned very close to her and called her one more vicious name. "Now bring me the money," he said.

Chelsea kept her calm. "You can't frighten me. Your words will never hurt me."

"Will fire?" asked her brother.

Chapter Ten

"Did you hear?" demanded Perky Palmer. Her light blue eyes gleamed with gossip. She considered her eyes her best asset. Most people disagreed. Perky's eyes reflected her ugly thoughts.

"Hear what?" said Dawn, not very interested. She was caught up in her own daydream. The dream was a mixture of Pete, Monty, and Gideon, of saving the world and dancing at the Chrystal Falls gala.

"The gazebo on the golf course," said Perky breathlessly, "was torched."

Dawn was confused. "Torched?"

They were in the library, supposedly working on their term papers. One class a week they left history for the library. Nobody had done anything yet except open the books. Dawn was so distracted her own book was upside down. Because the librarian was eyeing them, Karen Pickett carefully swung Dawn's book around so she would look more authentic. Karen smiled sweetly at Mrs. Finelli and said to Dawn, "Perky means the gazebo was set fire to. Arson. Somebody did it on purpose."

"The golf course at the country club?" gasped Dawn. "How awful!"

Karen shrugged. "Everybody's been waiting for it to happen. The minute we heard Monty Chrystal was around we knew it was only a matter of time."

"How can you draw a conclusion like that on absolutely no evidence?" Dawn cried. "I think you're terrible."

Karen just looked at her. "It is terrible, Dawn, but the terrible one isn't me. It's Monty."

Perky saw what was going to happen between them and loved it. She had resented Dawn from the instant she arrived — her and that tennis star brother of hers, moving in on Perky's territory, Dawn trying to be friends with Chelsea and leaving Perky out in the cold.

"Monty's no good," said Karen casually. "Never has been."

Dawn Newhouse slammed her open book shut. "What a town. Every time I get used to how you people think, I get another shock. So Monty raises a little hell at prep schools. So

138

big deal. You and Pete automatically consider him some kind of criminal. You don't have any evidence, Karen. You just choose to hate anybody from the Hill."

Perky smiled.

"That's not fair," said Karen hotly. "Monty used to be my brother's best friend. I know Monty, Dawn. He's sick."

"*I* think he's charming," said Dawn.

Even Perky was astonished at that line.

"Charming?" repeated Karen in disbelief.

Perky decided it was time to raise a little hell herself. She said to Dawn, "You're right, of course. Montgomery finally realized that hanging out with Johnnie Pickett was stupid. Of course the Mill people resent that. It was kind of an honor for them to have Montgomery around. Now they like to blame everything on Monty. It's nasty, but then, what can you expect?"

Karen could not believe Perky Palmer had said that out loud. Her hot temper flared and her fingers found her reference book — heavy and sharp-edged. "That's not true, Perky!" she spat out. "You are a congenital liar and everyone knows it. An honor for us to have Monty around? You're as sick as he is, Perky."

Perky shook her head and said to Dawn, "See what I mean?"

Karen flung the book in Perky's face. She was an athlete; she had good aim. The book landed flat against Perky's nose, and a spurt

of blood and a scream of pain and surprise
came with it.

Mrs. Finelli screamed, "What's going on?"

Perky clutched her face, screaming, "She
tried to kill me!"

In her attempt to stop Karen, Dawn fell
backwards onto Perky and they both hit the
table and then the floor. Perky screamed as
if they were murdering her. There were probably thirty or forty other kids in the library.
Every one of them leaped up and ran over
to the girls' table to see what was going on.

Mrs. Finelli dragged Dawn up. She was
trembling with anger. "Dawn Newhouse!" she
cried. "How could you start a fight like this?
Here you were cozying up to me about your
tutoring and all the time you're the kind of
girl who starts fist fights! I am truly shocked."

Dawn's jaw dropped. She stopped massaging
the arm on which she had fallen and said,
"Me? Now wait a minute. I—"

"Don't you argue with me!" screamed Mrs.
Finelli. She had to scream, because there were
forty other opinions being offered at the same
time. The place had turned into a madhouse
almost instantly. Karen had her hands over
her eyes. She could not believe she had done
this.

The vice-principal, whose office was next
door, entered the library on the run. Threatening every student with every conceivable
punishment, he had most of them back in

140

their seats quickly. "Who is at the bottom of this?" he demanded.

"Dawn Newhouse," said the librarian, who was still so angry she could hardly speak.

"I am not!" cried Dawn.

"Don't talk back to me," snapped Mrs. Finelli.

Karen said, "Listen, this was all my fault. Dawn was just —"

"Miss Pickett, do not interfere," said the vice-principal. He was showing off his ability to control rowdy students and he didn't want to let his big chance go by, thought Karen ruefully. A lot of rough kids were in the library and the vice-principal had a chance to look tough. Easy to do with Dawn. "I have Mrs. Finelli's version of what happened, and that is the version I accept. Miss Newhouse, you will come with me to my office."

Karen tried to argue, and then tried to follow, but gave up. Mrs. Finelli put her arms around Perky, whose nose was fine with the help of one Kleenex, and comforted her. Perky made the most of it. Karen could not imagine why Perky didn't say what had really happened. Perky had always detested Karen. Why not get Karen into trouble, when Karen so richly deserved it?

But Perky was enjoying the attention she was getting, especially when a boy she liked got into the act, agreeing to walk her gently to the nurse.

Karen thought, I knew Perky was jealous of Dawn, but I didn't know she was *that* jealous!

In the hallway, Dawn walked beside the vice-principal. She was overcome with humiliation and fury. She — the best behaved of anyone — was in trouble. No doubt there would be detention, and for fighting in school, who knew? Perhaps she would even be suspended!

Her mother would be telephoned at the hospital. Wonderful. She had planned to save the world and so far all she had accomplished was to give her mother another severe headache. Her mother would be so ashamed!

Sure enough. Loss of library privileges, which meant getting her term paper done was going to be rather difficult. And detention for a week. That meant patrolling the school grounds, picking up cigarette butts and candy wrappers from the weeds along the fences.

"I did not do anything," said Dawn two more times, glaring at the vice-principal. I hate you, she thought. You won't even listen to me. This must be how Montgomery Chrystal feels. Blamed by habit. Something happens — it must be Monty — let's drag his name into it.

Oh, the injustice of this town! she thought, beginning to cry. Chrystal Falls breeds gossip the way some climates breed mosquitoes. Well, from now on, I am one hundred percent on Monty's side. I don't care what lies they tell. I will understand what it's like to be blamed for something you didn't do.

The vice-principal dismissed her just as passing bell rang for the next class. Of course, everyone in the library had been at work telling what had happened up there, and in moments it seemed to Dawn the entire population of the school knew.

"Hey, criminal!" yelled one of the girls from French, laughing. "Got detention, huh?" The other girls with her laughed hysterically.

Dawn, who normally loved the world, hated her classmates. She answered nobody, but trudged to her next class. And then Pete came running up to her. Literally running down the halls, weaving among the kids, virtually pushing the slow movers out of the way.

His arms were around her. "Are you all right?" he said anxiously.

The anxiety in his voice destroyed the rest of her composure. Dawn burst into tears. He had no books and hers were still in the library so their arms were free, and they wrapped themselves in each other, oblivious to the cheers and remarks of their classmates. "I heard Perky started throwing things," he said. "I wasn't sure who got the bloody nose."

"No, no," said Dawn, "it was *Karen* who threw things. Karen was telling lies about Monty Chrystal, and Perky —"

"*Karen* told lies?" said Pete. "Impossible. Anyway, nobody could lie about Monty. The only truth is that he's dirt."

Dawn drew back from Pete, looking at him queerly. Pete knew she was upset with him, but couldn't imagine why. He said, "Listen. I don't know what the quarrel was about, but I promise you, Karen was the one telling the truth."

"Why do you promise?" said Dawn coldly. "Because you feel Mill people are always good and Hill people are always bad?"

"Oh, don't start that again," said Pete in exasperation.

"I didn't start anything!" cried Dawn. "You people always start it. You and all your prejudices."

Pete was simply confused. But he loved her and he was worried about her, and after the arson on the golf course he knew that the important thing was that she must not go back to Halfway House. He said, "Whatever. It doesn't matter. The thing is, Dawn, you've got to quit tutoring Gideon. I don't want you back at Halfway House. Monty's up to his old tricks and it isn't safe. I was willing to let you try it, but now I can't let you go back."

Dawn stepped away from him. She thought, Less than sixty seconds ago I loved you. Now my love has died as if it had never been. "You won't *let* me?" she repeated. "You were *willing* at first, but now you won't *let* me?"

Pete knew a strategic error when he heard one. "Sorry," he said quickly. "I didn't mean that. It's just that you have to understand that Monty — "

"I understand that you are one of the most narrow-minded people I have ever known," she said, and the tears came stronger and harder. Passing period was coming to an end. There were fewer witnesses. Pete had no idea what to do. "Where's your brother?" he said at last. "Maybe he can talk some sense into you."

It was the last straw for Dawn. The very idea! She began screaming at Pete. Pete tried to silence her, knowing if she got a second warning in one day, she'd get suspended from school. Dawn — who was so sweet! Desperately he tried to tell her how her thinking had gotten twisted, but all he did was get himself into deeper waters.

Out of the corner of his eye he saw Chelsea Chrystal sauntering toward them. Pete Carter had little use for Chelsea. She was a rich snob whose family traditionally used those around them, and she was no exception.

But in a pinch, Chelsea would be honorable. Dawn had to stay away from Montgomery Chrystal and the only person who was in a position to make her see reason was Monty's sister.

145

"Chelsea!" yelled Pete Carter. "Chelsea, I need you."

It was the worst day of Chelsea Chrystal's life. The princess of Chrystal Falls was not immune to gossip. If anything, she received more of it. The fire that took the gazebo was regarded as Monty's fault and secondarily her parents' and grandparents'. Nobody knew that it was partially Chelsea's fault, for this was the first step in Monty's warning to her to bring the money. She was sick with horror that he had done this, and sicker with the knowledge that she came into it.

And there was no Josh to comfort her. No Josh to turn to. He was gone. She felt amputated. They had known each other well for such a short time, and yet she counted on him. Needed him.

When Chelsea walked into the bathroom, two girls applying makeup in front of the mirrors were saying, "You'd think those Chrystals would have enough love for our town to lock him up. Imagine letting that dirt Monty run around loose."

"He isn't actually loose, Anne. He's at Half-way House."

"Same thing as loose. Monty Chrystal should be behind bars."

"Oh, hi, Chelsea." A sugary-sweet voice that slurped over her and made her sick. "Didn't see you walk in," said Anne.

146

Oh, sure, thought Chelsea.

. . . and when she was in lunch line even the cooks were talking about it. As they dished out macaroni and cheese, one said, "That pretty little gazebo. All that filigree woodwork and those nice rose bushes that flowered in June. What'll he torch next?"

"More of the country club," said the other cook. "Hates his own kind, I guess. Makes you glad you're not Hill people."

The first cook sniffed. "Blood runs thin in that family. Nothing much to this generation. You watch. The mill's going to go right down the tubes."

That's me, thought Chelsea. She means me. There's nothing much to my generation. Trembling, she went to a table without getting lunch. Ryan was waiting for her. Good old Ryan. But Ryan's house was among the ones vandalized a year ago and Ryan could not resist saying, "Your dear brother's up to his old tricks, huh?"

She was eaten by shame.

Next to him sat Ian MacFarland. He had been Chelsea's friend since they toddled to nursery school together. He said, "You call that a trick? I call arson a crime."

She had to sit with them. There was no place else to go. If I had just brought Monty the money he asked for, this wouldn't have happened, she thought. He'd be gone. We'd be free of him. No wonder my family always

147

gives in to Monty! A match is powerful. A fire destroys your soul as well as a building.

Oh, Josh, how could you have left me for your tennis? she thought dismally. Now — when I need you.

And yet, did she need to have him hear any of this?

Ian and Ryan talked about the fracas in the library. Chelsea paid no attention. She left the lunch room early and walked the halls. She was startled to have Pete Carter call her name. Pete — to whom she never spoke.

"Chelsea, I need you!"

He was standing by Dawn. Was Dawn hurt?

Momentarily forgetting her own family, Chelsea rushed over to help. But whatever the pain was, it wasn't physical. Dawn was standing like a child who had been whipped and Pete looked as if he felt responsible. Well, that's one good thing, thought Chelsea grimly. That silly relationship is over. If Pete thinks I'm going to mend it, he's out of his mind.

"Oh, Chelsea," said Dawn, "how can you stand this town? People are terrible here."

Chelsea said nothing. The most terrible person was her own brother.

"Poor Monty," said Dawn next. Chelsea's heart sank. She looked at Pete and the look he gave her back was unmistakable.

"They were accusing Monty of arson," said Dawn, "and they had nothing to go on. Not a shred of evidence. But they didn't care about evidence. They just assumed it was Monty. I don't know how you can stand living in Chrystal Falls, Chelsea."

Chelsea could not speak. Her rotten brother had torched a building and sweet, gentle Dawn was protecting him.

Uttering Pete's name as if it were a swear word, Dawn went on, "And *Pete* says he won't *let* me tutor Gideon because he won't *let* me be around Monty."

Chelsea closed her eyes. Pete was absolutely right. There was no argument on Dawn's side and every argument against her.

All right, thought Chelsea, right now I have to admit it. In front of all these kids, in front of Pete. Yes, Dawn, do as Pete says because I'm sorry to say he's right. He's not being a male trying to dominate you, and he's not being Hill/Mill. He's just right.

But the words did not come out. A combination of pride in herself and family loyalty, of hatred for Monty and hatred for herself at not being able to beat Monty — all these surfaced, and Chelsea said, "It's nice of you to be on the side of justice, Dawn."

Pete sucked in his breath.

Chelsea looked at him. Utter contempt looked back.

What have I done? thought Chelsea.

Pete turned on his heel to leave. There was still time to retrieve things. Now, before Pete stormed off, Chelsea could retract her words. Could admit the truth.

But she didn't.

And Pete left them both, Dawn crying, Chelsea frozen.

Bells rang. Dawn rushed to her class. Chelsea remained numbed in the middle of the corridor.

And then she, too, ran. Out of school, into her car, onto the road — anything to get away from what was happening to her.

I hate my life! thought Chelsea, as the tears came at last, blinding her, making it hard to drive. The boy I love left me, the family I love deserted me. Everything is wrong, nothing will ever be right.

And I did the wrong thing and it makes me sick.

She stopped at a major intersection. The light went green, but she didn't move, in spite of honking cars behind her. She just sat, weeping, unable to think where she should turn.

And then she thought, Why don't I do what Amy said to do? I can go to New York by myself. For that matter, I could go to London or Paris by myself. My whole family runs away or hides. Why can't I?

And Monty's right. I do have lots of money.

She sat through another light change, honking drivers passing her with difficulty.

And then she turned left, and drove to Chrystal Falls Airport.

150

Chapter Eleven

Airports invariably filled Chelsea with excitement. The constantly moving, demanding passengers sent a thrill of urgency through her, and the uniforms of the airline personnel sparked her sense of adventure. As she entered the terminal, elbowed by half-running passengers afraid of missing their flights, a plane took off. White with scarlet stripes, like a cheerleading uniform, it rose into the gray sky, a splinter of adventure, circled triumphantly, and spun into the horizon.

Chelsea shivered with delight.

I haven't even got a change of clothing, she thought. I'll have to buy clothes when I get to New York. And luggage. And shampoo and makeup.

A fresh start.

Everything new. Everything different.

The only pang she felt was for Josh, but even he seemed too distant to worry about. She walked to the first ticket counter and asked about the next flight to New York.

"Our next flight isn't for another four hours," said the pleasant woman in the striking uniform, "but if you're in a hurry the other airline has a flight boarding right this minute, and they may have space left."

"I'm in a hurry," agreed Chelsea, and she *was* in a hurry, but whether to leave Chrystal Falls or to start a new life, she wasn't sure. Running across the carpeted room to the other line, she bought a ticket with one of her credit cards, was directed to gate nine and told to hurry even more.

The hurrying added to the excitement. It was part of air travel that you rushed. The importance of getting there *now* took precedence over everything else.

A relaxed stewardess welcomed her aboard and ushered her into a seat in the smoking section, which Chelsea detested, but there was nothing else available. She had no sooner buckled her seat belt than the plane began taxiing onto the runway.

Next to her a businessman her father's age opened a briefcase and began looking at a folder of statistics. Across the aisle a businesswoman in a lovely dark red suit opened a paperback and read quietly. Chelsea, in the window seat, gripped the arm of her chair and, as the plane rose into the air, stared down at the town she was abandoning.

They circled above Rapid River, a curl of silver among the houses, mills, and forests. There were the roofs and smokestacks of Chrystal Mills, which were partly hers. The high school was hidden by the wing of the plane, but the track field made a neat tan oval, like some prehistoric designs drawn by a primitive person to impress some god.

The hospital was marked out by its four wings, spread in a great cross not too far from the river. Chelsea thought of hospitals, and of Dr. Newhouse, and then of Josh, and she thought, *What am I doing?*

The small city vanished.

Now they flew over dim gray and green forests, and then rose into the clouds and flew silently in the thick mistiness of late winter.

Never had Chelsea Chrystal made a decision so quickly. In less than forty-five minutes, she had abandoned all the pressures of her home and town. She had left Pete's scorn and Dawn's future; she had left her mother's terrors and Monty's demands; she had left Amy to fend for herself; she had left Josh to come back from the tennis tournament to find himself a prince of the courts without a princess to date.

It was such an enormous decision. She could not even focus on it. Out her window there was nothing but the wing and the clouds. Chelsea sat, astonished and numb, and looked into the ocean of gray.

Monty Chrystal paced the yard at Halfway House. He was pleased with how he had dealt with the police. He knew his rights. And good old George Palmer, attorney at law, had stood by with advice. Naturally neither his mother nor father had come. But it hardly mattered. The message had been for Chelsea, and his sister would arrive after school with the money. And if she didn't . . . well, he would take his rage out on somebody, that was for sure.

Dawn wanted to skip her detention and go home and cry for a few hours. Whenever she thought of Pete her heart hurt. It was like battling knives in her chest: a true cutting pain. Pete, whom she adored!

But the Hill kids had been right, in the end. Pete was like all the other Mill kids. He couldn't see past his prejudices. It would never have worked out.

And yet Dawn wanted to run to Pete and fling herself upon him, and take comfort from him. She could feel how his hands had lightly caressed her hair, those nights when she walked the dog and he came with her, and they wandered in the chill of the dark down toward the river, and talked of painful things, like homesickness, and good things, like each other.

Comfort, she thought. As if he'd offer comfort to me now. He thinks I've committed the crime of being a Hill person.

If only her brother Josh was in town! He would have to have this tennis stuff just when she needed him.

Loneliness settled in Dawn's heart like something solid and immoveable.

She thought of Monty. How lonely *he* must be! She would see him this afternoon, after detention, and let him know that not everybody in this dreadful town was relentlessly cruel. And perhaps Monty would have some words of comfort for her, too, because he had been through it all.

The gym teacher noticed Chelsea's absence and reported it. She was the daughter of a mill hand herself, and always resented Chelsea's belief that she could wiggle out of things. She just doesn't want to do volleyball, thought the gym teacher. She's bad at it, and she hates doing anything she's bad at, so she's cutting class. Well, for once Miss Chrystal won't get away with it.

The gym teacher sent a message up to the office to report Chelsea's cut.

Pete Carter cut class, too. He felt like talking to Mitch, who was in gym, so he changed into gym shorts and joined Mitch's class,

which was running laps around the baseball
fields. The coach never noticed another body
in the class. Pete ran alongside Mitch, who
laughed. "What're you doing here?" said
Mitch.

"Cutting. Too mad to sit still." He told
Mitch what had happened with Dawn and
Chelsea.

Mitch shook his head. "Don't fool around
with Dawn. She's a nice girl and all, and she's
pretty, but sometimes I don't think she's got
her head screwed on straight."

These were precisely Pete's own thoughts,
and yet when Mitch said this out loud, Pete
felt like kicking him. He tried to defend
Dawn, saying that all this Hill/Mill garbage
had confused her, but what he really felt was
a desperation he could not express to Mitch: a
feeling that he could not stand it if he lost
Dawn.

And he knew that he had lost her.

In the school office, a very bored secretary
looked at the lists of class cutters and debated
calling the parents. It was hard to reach people; they were all at work, and a lot of them
didn't care if their kids cut class or not.

Chelsea Chrystal.

Well, that was a name that had never appeared on the cut list before! And that was a
parent who definitely was not at work!

The secretary didn't feel like calling Mrs.

Chrystal, however. The elegance and wealth of the family made her uncomfortable. She hated interrupting them. Besides, everybody was talking about the son, who was some sick arsonist they were all afraid of. The secretary didn't think she wanted to tangle with that crowd.

And in the air, coming into LaGuardia Airport, Chelsea Chrystal swallowed nervously. Roads were visible as they descended. She could see the basketball hoop on the playground of a city school, and make out the dotted white lines of the parkways.

Her hands were damp, and it was not fear of landing. It was fear of what she would do after she landed. The crush of exiting passengers swept her off the plane, through the moveable corridor, and into the terminal, but she did not go downstairs with the rest to the baggage claim. Instead she walked up a wide, crowded ramp into the main terminal.

She had been dressing well for school since Monty's return. The fine clothes were a protection, the way jeans could never be. In a gray skirt and mauve jacket, she was slim and elegant, her dark gold hair a cap of beauty and her posture an exhibit of assurance.

A sharp but slow-spoken voice came over loudspeakers, very carefully enunciating a change in flight plans. Chelsea stared into the window of a candy shop. "At three-oh-eight,"

157

said the voice, and then repeated the time twice more.

School in Chrystal Falls had been out since two forty-five.

Dawn would be going to detention. Detention would end at three forty-five. Dawn had a car because Josh was away, and Dr. Newhouse walked to work at the hospital.

There's no point in thinking about them, Chelsea told herself. First, I need clothes. There aren't any clothing shops in the airport. I should take a limousine into Manhattan, spend the first day shopping, and fly abroad tomorrow.

In Chrystal Falls, Dawn Newhouse walked the border of the school grounds, carrying a long stick with a sharp metal prong on it. Stabbing bits of litter and stuffing it into her plastic trash bag, Dawn made her way around the field. Two very skanky low-life boys also had the chore. She was afraid of them.

This horrid town! How had she ever thought she could find any happiness in Chrystal Falls!

She thought of Pete Carter, and blinked back a rush of tears.

"Mitch, come with me. Please," begged Karen Pickett.

"I'd come with you to the ends of the earth," said Mitch, kissing her.

Pete Carter grinned at his friends. "Don't listen to that guy," Pete told Karen. "Mitch won't go past the city lines of Chrystal Falls. Even for you."

"I did remember to tell you that after we're married we're going to live in Manhattan, didn't I?" Karen teased, kissing Mitch back.

"Yes, you did," said Mitch. "And I'm drawing up a petition for the city of Chrystal Falls right now. They're going to rename A Avenue Manhattan Avenue."

The trio laughed, but only Mitch really thought it was funny.

"Now where are we going?" Mitch wanted to know.

"The principal's office. I have to straighten out this mess with Dawn and Perky," Karen explained.

"That girl's a nut case," Mitch observed. "Making friends with Monty. Unreal."

"She isn't a nut case," Karen said. "She's a very nice, decent person and if the Hill had more of her, Chrystal Falls would be a better town. She just doesn't understand about Monty. She gets an idea in her head and crowbars won't get it out."

Pete wished the idea Dawn had in her head was him. Romance, love, sex. But the idea she was hooked on now was Monty Chrystal's innocence.

It took quite a while to bring the principal around. He, like Mrs. Finelli, was sure that

Perky, daughter of fine, upstanding George Palmer, was more believable than any trio of Mill kids. All the evidence was against Perky. Her lying and holding back had nearly given Mitch a jail sentence last year. And yet, here was the principal seeing only her money and status and clothing and believing Perky first and Karen last.

Twice Mitch touched Karen's shoulder to remind her not to lose her temper again. Finally the principal conceded that Dawn had done nothing wrong. Mitch and Pete walked Karen out of the office before she told the principal what she thought of him.

"Let's go out and tell Dawn," said Karen.

"No," said Mitch, "they'll go get her. I don't want another argument about Monty Chrystal. We've got better things to do."

"That's true," said Karen. "Mother finished my dress. I want you to come to my house and I'll try it on for you."

"I'd rather you took it off for me," said Mitch.

They giggled, kidding each other, Dawn and Monty and even Pete who stood next to them entirely forgotten. They drove off in Mitch's car, leaving Pete standing uncertainly at the school.

Pete stared out across the wide lawns, through the winter silhouettes of the bare trees, as Dawn's tiny figure bent and straightened over bits of invisible trash.

160

But he didn't know what to say to her to make things right, or to change her mind. A cold wind lifted his jacket and he shivered slightly and went to his own car and drove away.

Chapter Twelve

Dawn kept thinking of her father. What a gap had been left in the Newhouse family when Daddy died so young. He wouldn't be mad at me over this detention, Dawn thought. He'd laugh and straighten it all out and he'd do it so nicely we'd all end up buddies.

If only she had a buddy right now. It was a second-grade sort of word. A comforting word.

Dawn made a list of friends in her mind. Pete, who made her pulse race and her speech stutter, was not a buddy. Her feelings for him were too complicated: sex mixed with confusion, love mixed with anger. Chelsea? No, Chelsea would never be anybody's buddy. A shining star, but not a buddy. Karen was funny and crazy and great company, but too prickly to be a buddy. Josh? An older brother can understand only so much. Besides, Josh had been out of it lately. Dawn did not know if it was tennis, a girl, or something she was totally unaware of in his life. It made her uneasy, not knowing.

Dawn walked over damp, raw fields back to the office. Her bag was full of cigarette butts and crushed soft drink cans. The principal tossed it into his trash can and had the grace to look ashamed. "Karen Pickett was here," he said. "She explained what really happened. I believe everybody just flew off the handle and we're simply going to forget the entire episode."

Dawn stared at him. "Why didn't you call me back the moment you realized I didn't deserve the punishment?" she asked.

"Well, I was getting to it, but I had some calls to make first," said the principal. He smiled very brightly.

You toad, thought Dawn Newhouse. You didn't care that I was cold and crying and afraid of those skanks out there with me. You were too lazy to bother coming for me.

Never had she felt so completely and so unfairly used.

She walked out of the office, wishing she could walk out of Chrystal Falls, too, and drove to Halfway House. The bleak sky had darkened early and tall, grim evergreens closed in around Halfway House like prison walls. Who could be happy here? she thought, forgetting the kind Sheffields and the way the glass porch gleamed in the sun.

She had barely turned off the ignition — in fact, her fingers were still clinging to the key ring — when the passenger door opened. Startled, Dawn whirled in her seat. "Monty!" she said. "You surprised me."

"Sorry about that." He flashed the Chrystal smile at her, and it worked for him the way it did so often, charming her entirely.

Never had Dawn needed to talk so much, and the words spilled out of her. "You'll never guess what happened to me today," she told Monty, turning in her seat to face him. She wanted to cry, but didn't. Monty raised his eyebrows, looking sympathetic, and Dawn told him her whole story.

Monty kept his face still. He could not care less what happened to her or anybody else in Chrystal Falls. He nodded at the appropriate times and the story went on and on. He thought, Chelsea isn't here. School's been out over an hour, and she didn't bring me money. I set fire to that gazebo and still she didn't knuckle under.

Dawn talked about justice.

Stupid girl. There was no such thing as justice. Monty thought, I could just take this car. But she probably doesn't have any money. It made him mad that the only car available to him belonged to this silly girl, whining about justice. It made him madder that the girl didn't even have money. It made him absolutely furious that Chelsea had not come.

Dawn told him that her boyfriend had not understood her. Monty knew it had to be Pete Carter. He had hated Pete Carter since nursery school. "I'll be your buddy," said Monty warmly.

She gave him a smile of pure gratitude.

He said, "You need a rest. Let me drive. We'll just go for a spin and take your mind off things."

"Is it all right for you to leave?" said Dawn anxiously.

"Sure," he said. "The Sheffields know I didn't have anything to do with that terrible fire on the golf course."

"Oh, I'm so glad!" she cried. "I knew they were good people."

Monty said, "Oh, they're wonderful." He got out, walked around the car, and slid into the driver's seat as Dawn slid across to the passenger side. He turned on the engine. The rush of power beneath his feet excited him. He had no money; he had no escape. But he had a car with a powerful engine, and he could drive: drive fast, drive far, maybe hit something, maybe crush something.

Anything to release the terrible anger that was building in him, moment by moment.

Elizabeth Chrystal said to the school secretary, "My daughter cut class? That doesn't

165

sound like her. Are you sure?"

"We're sure," said the secretary dryly, thinking, I knew it. I knew she'd accuse me of making a mistake, instead of darling Chelsea of cutting.

Both women hung up gratefully. Elizabeth Chrystal had not answered a phone in days and the touch with the real world left her trembling. How odd that Chelsea had cut class! She never did that!

In her place, thought Elizabeth Chrystal, I would run away.

We didn't help her. We shoved all our problems onto her shoulders. I didn't help her with the big things — like facing an entire town when Monty came back. And I didn't help her with the smaller things — like getting a dress for the mall opening.

The phone rang again and she seized it quickly, hoping it was Chelsea, praying it was Chelsea — but it was Halfway House.

Monty was gone.

Hundreds of miles away, Chelsea stood leaning against a blank wall, staring across the terminal at a bank of telephones. They were not in booths with doors that closed, but in slots, without privacy or protection from the racket of the airport. Most were empty. She had a credit card; she didn't even need change.

She knew today was Dawn's day at Halfway

House. Right now Dawn was there. Right now she was talking to Monty. A Monty who would be furious because Chelsea had not appeared with money. He had set fire to the gazebo. What would he do next? Not fire again. If fire hadn't frightened Chelsea enough, what would? Dawn. Monty would stop at nothing . . . and he had Dawn with him now. Chelsea shivered. She knew Monty too well and knew who he would attack next. Dawn.

I ran, thought Chelsea. The cooks at school were right. The blood ran thin in this generation of Chrystals. First sign of pressure and I skipped.

What will Josh think of me?

He would think of only one thing — that Chelsea had had a chance to stop Dawn from associating with Monty, and Chelsea chose not to tell the truth.

Josh will despise me, thought Chelsea. I won't be his princess. I'll be an object of loathing. There will be a dance and if I go, nobody will speak to me; and if I don't, I'll be hiding from what I've done. Allowing Dawn to be in a position of terrible danger.

She called her mother — and the line was busy.

She called the Newhouse apartment — and there was no answer.

She did not waste time calling her father. He would insist on getting hold of George

Palmer and getting legal advice first, and by that time God knew what Monty might have done to Dawn.

Chelsea Chrystal made the toughest decision of her life. She rang up Pennsylvania information and got the number of the Chrystal Falls Police Department. She had to take action, and if it meant turning in her own brother, so be it.

She did not know that the person who hated her right then was not Josh but Pete Carter. Pete drove aimlessly around Chrystal Falls, torn apart with worry and love. He cruised down A Avenue. Mitch's car was at Karen's. Pete decided to join them. He didn't want to bring up the subject of Dawn, but maybe Karen would. He really wanted to talk about it. Or at least, to hear someone else talk about it.

Pete opened the front door and yelled hello.

"We're right here," said Karen from the couch on his right. "You don't have to scream."

Mitch removed his arm from Karen's shoulders. "Come on in, even if you are interrupting everything."

Pete came in. He wished he was sitting in the Newhouse living room with his arm around Dawn like that, but he wasn't, and he didn't know what to do about it.

"Karen's about to try on her dress for me,"

said Mitch. "Sit down. Have a ringside seat. Her dress is even going to outshine Chelsea's from New York."

"Terrific," said Pete, who could not care less what anybody wore to the mall opening, especially since he wouldn't be going with Dawn now. "Show it off, Karen."

Karen slipped into her bedroom and drew from the padded hanger the dress her mother had almost finished. Only the hemline wasn't complete, just basted down. Until they bought matching shoes, they weren't sure just where it should fall. Tugging off layers of shirts, Karen tossed her jeans into the laundry and kicked her sneakers aside. She stood in front of the long mirror in her bra and pants. She was a small girl, and slim and perfectly proportioned. She liked everything she saw. She kept watching as she slipped into the gown. She eased the zipper up, caught the hook and eye, and wriggled slightly so the fabric would fall perfectly.

Oh, those colors!

Slipping and sliding into each other in a blaze of vibrant shapes, they turned her from a high school girl into a dazzling woman. She looked mysterious above that shimmering neckline, and her dark eyes mocked her, as though they belonged to the woman in the mirror, and not to Karen Pickett of Chrystal Falls.

World, here I come!

169

A triumphant expression caught the corners of her lips and she laughed out loud at the sight of herself. Behind her the gown swirled. Running a brush through her hair — it always fell the same, a thick, dark adornment to her delicate features — she added lip gloss and went out to show the boys. The silken cloth whispered over her bare legs.

How incongruous she was in that cramped, dark living room!

A Avenue was a row of identical millworkers' houses built generations ago. The trees and shrubs had grown up to soften the yards and porches, but nothing would make the small room handsome.

Mitch thought that Karen was the most beautiful woman he had ever seen. He usually thought of her as his girl, and the word *woman* startled him and made him uncertain. She did not look like Chrystal Falls. She looked too special, too dramatic.

Out of place.

He was terribly proud of her, but slightly unnerved. He could not speak the words she wanted to hear.

Pete said them out loud: how lovely she was, how lovely the dress. He thought that Karen belonged on a stage. Not a stage with audience and props, but the stage of a bigger life — a New York or a Chicago. She was tough, Karen was, and Pete had always admired it in her.

You're right, Karen, he thought, but he did not say it out loud because Mitch wouldn't care for it. You have to leave this mill town. You have more to offer than it will ever have to give you.

Karen pirouetted for them.

Mitch, who had done no ballroom dancing in his entire life, put his hands out in the proper way, one resting lightly on her waist, and the other holding her extended hand in a graceful sweep to the side.

They danced to no music but the music of their love.

Pete could hardly watch.

I won't dance with Dawn, he thought. She'll go with some twit like Ryan Simpson and I won't go at all.

At last Mitch and Karen broke apart, the spell between them still intense, but moving in private directions that Pete could not share. "I have to hang the dress back up," she said softly to Mitch. They kissed so lightly that Pete knew they were forcing themselves not to kiss with the passion they really felt.

Karen left the room. Both boys watched her walk, the hips undulating under the vivid silk, and sighed for what they didn't yet have.

For a few moments they sat silently on the faded flowery couch in the Pickett living room. To change the subject, Mitch said casually, "We saw Dawn riding around with Monty this afternoon."

"You what?" said Pete, shocked.

"In Dawn's car. But Monty was driving. We slowed down to see. You know Monty. I actually had visions of Monty kidnapping her, silly as that sounds."

It didn't sound silly to Pete Carter.

"But she was smiling at him," Mitch went on. "Never saw us. I guess Hill is better than Mill even when Hill is insane."

"The zipper is stuck," Karen called from the bedroom. "Come undo it for me. Mother will kill me if I tear the fabric."

Mitch leaped up from the couch, always willing to unzip Karen.

Pete leaped up even faster, but his reason was very different.

Dawn — with Monty?

As the sky darkened and a cold winter night fell?

Monty, who was not allowed off the grounds of Halfway House?

He saw at last that this had nothing to do with Hill and Mill. This was a case of a lovely girl who believed in justice and thought she was on the right side. She'll get hurt, thought Pete.

And it was not emotional hurt he was thinking of. It was what Monty could do to her.

"Karen!" he yelled.

"I'm not dressed yet, Pete."

"Where did Monty and your brother Johnnie used to hang out?"

There was a startled silence. "He used to buy his drugs from some dealer with a cabin in the woods over by Lost Bridge," said Karen. "Sometimes they'd fish there, and drink beer."

It was a long shot.

Monty could have driven anywhere.

But Pete believed that Monty was a creature of habit — that he had his home territories and his techniques — like the burning of a building.

Pete was out the door and in his car, backing out of the short drive, and racing through the late afternoon traffic without regard for rules of safety.

Let me get there first, he thought.

Chapter Thirteen

"Thank you, Miss Chrystal," said the official voice. "We've already been notified by several people. A general search is on."

Chelsea thanked him, too, and hung up, staring at the bustle of LaGuardia Airport around her. Several people did the right thing before I did, she thought. Despair seized her. One last time she tried the Chrystal mansion and this time she got through. "Oh, Mother!" she cried, dissolving at the sound of that voice.

"Chelsea, sweetheart, where are you?" said her mother instantly. "I'll come get you."

"I'm at LaGuardia," said Chelsea.

Her mother gasped. "In New York?"

"I was going to go to Paris or London."

Her mother managed a laugh. "Your passport is in my desk," she reminded her daughter. "And it's a long way to go for a dress. I'm going to call Lavinia. You take a limousine into Manhattan and stay with her. She'll find you a dress and put you on a plane back here."

"Oh, Mother, I don't care about the dress! I've done the most terrible thing." The shameful story of not telling Dawn the truth poured out of Chelsea. Never had she carried so much guilt.

"I know, honey," said her mother gently. "But don't be too hard on yourself. Our whole family is guilty. None of us could bear to admit who and what Monty is. But now we have to face it."

"Mother, it isn't just a question of facing it! Dawn is probably with him right now! He could hurt her."

They were silent. They knew Monty better than anyone.

"We'll just have to hope the police find them first," said Mrs. Chrystal finally.

"That's not very comforting," said Chelsea, sobbing.

"There's nothing you can do now," her mother said. "Just go to Lavinia's and — "

"But there was plenty I could have done then!" cried Chelsea.

There was a long quiet. "I hid in my room," said her mother at last. "I won't do it again. But we're all guilty."

Admitting guilt, thought Chelsea, is all very well. But it doesn't save Dawn.

* * *

Dawn did not recognize the roads. Monty had left the town by crossing the new bridge — so-called although it had been up for decades — and turning south. "Where are we?" said Dawn. There weren't street lights here.

Monty didn't answer her.

"Where are we headed?" she said uneasily. Her chatter had run down. She was aware that Monty had not answered her since he began driving.

The warning that people had given her about Monty began to surface, like little needles pricking Dawn's mind.

Monty turned to the right without slowing for the curve. Not having fixed her seat belt, Dawn was thrown against him. He grinned at her, driving faster still. What a queer grin. What a strange twist it gave to his Chrystal features. His eyes had a funny cast, as if there was something wrong with the brain behind them.

The edge of panic touched Dawn. Goose bumps lifted on her fair skin.

Monty stopped the car very quickly. It had power brakes, and they grabbed, tossing Dawn against the dashboard.

Monty laughed when she moaned.

She was bruised but not seriously hurt. But when she raised her head and looked at Monty, she saw a different boy. Gone was the heavyset, sulky young man whose problems had made her so sympathetic. In his place sat the sick man who must indeed, as everyone had said, have set fire to the gazebo.

What have I done? thought Dawn.

Oh, Pete! she thought, wanting to be back in that school hallway, in the circle of his comforting arm. Why didn't I listen to you? Why was I angry with you instead of seeing Monty for what he is? Why didn't I realize you were thinking of *me* — not of Hill people?

She knew where they were now. As the last dim light of the sun darkened, she recognized Lost Bridge. Many years ago a hurricane flood had ripped it off. Rebuilding had occurred upstream. Now the bridge was nothing but a drop-off over dreadful, steep cliffs, with impenetrable dark woods all around the abandoned roads.

Monty leaned forward, his blazing eyes boring into hers. His laugh rose — a laugh of hatred and rage.

Dawn ripped her door open, getting out so fast she fell onto the pavement. Monty, still laughing, slid across the front seat to follow her.

Pete Carter had never driven like this. Accustomed to trucks and pick-ups, where extra care had to be taken, he was not the kind of boy who drove recklessly. This is the time a cop will stop me, he thought grimly, when I *have* to drive like this.

But no one saw him.

He was over the new bridge, taking the turn without bothering to come to a full stop. The tires screamed like sirens on the curves of the old river road. Across the river, rows and rows of light illuminated the second shift working at the factories.

And ahead of him, yards from the broken edge of Lost Bridge, was the unmistakable shape of Dawn's car. Pete leaned on his horn — a jarring, screaming noise. He couldn't see either Monty or Dawn, but this would let Dawn know somebody was coming, and it would let Monty know that this somebody meant business.

Monty was a bully — always had been. That meant he was more easily scared than you might think.

At the last moment Pete threw on his brakes, and it was a good thing he did. In front of his wheels were Monty and Dawn. Dawn was on the ground and Monty was bending over her. The headlights bathed them in a terrible picture of fear and attack. Dawn was slamming her fists against Monty's chest and screaming, "Don't! Don't!"

Flinging himself from the car, Pete pulled Monty away from Dawn. Monty was quick. He fled into the night, along the paths he knew so well at the cliff's edge.

Pete knelt beside Dawn, his knees hurting on the rough pebbles, his hands feverishly seeking reassurance that she was not hurt. "Oh, Pete!" she cried, her hands closing over his arms, her fingers tightening with relief. "Oh, Pete, I was so stupid. Thank God you came."

"Are you all right?" he said, scooping her up.

"Yes. He just scared me. Nothing happened." She wept now, tears streaming down her cheeks.

Pete marveled at Monty's luck. Once again, nothing had happened. Monty had committed no crime, had done nothing to be tried for, had simply frightened a girl who went along with him willingly.

I hope he falls off the cliff, Pete thought. It would solve a lot of people's problems.

Sirens cut through the night air. The police, too, knew Monty's habits, having followed them for many years. The Sheffields had not been paralyzed like the Chrystals. They had called immediately.

Dawn went so limp in Pete's arms he thought she had fainted. "No," she said almost inaudibly. "I'm just so tired."

He kissed her hair, hugged her yet again, and sat her down on the passenger side of his car, the door open.

"I'm the stupidest person in the world," she said.

"Oh, there's probably somebody stupider on the globe," teased Pete, "maybe out in the

179

Pacific Islands somewhere. But in .Chrystal Falls, no. You've got the honor sewed up."

Dawn said, "I didn't trust you."

Pete looked away from her. "No," he said. "And that hurt. I was worried about you. I wasn't trying to push you around."

The police were there immediately, thinking first that it was Monty holding Dawn, ready to rip him away. "Pete Carter," the boy identified himself. "Monty ran down the riverside paths."

The police turned on searchlights to look for Monty, and left Pete and Dawn alone in the dark once more.

"You saved my life," she said to him, her voice catching.

"I don't think so," said Pete. "Monty is bad, but I don't think he would have killed you. I know what he had in mind, but I can't believe he would have murdered you."

Dawn pressed against Pete. How comforting he was! Perhaps he really would be the buddy she sought! And friend, and boyfriend, too.

She said, "Why didn't Chelsea tell me?"

Pete had lived in Chrystal Falls all his life. He understood Chelsea and the rest of her family, even if he detested them. He could have said *pride*, but he didn't. He didn't want Dawn, whom he adored, to be friends with Chelsea. He said, "She thinks only of herself."

Dawn shuddered.

Pete thought, We're not going to stand here talking about Chelsea Chrystal, that's for sure. He said, "So, listen! Are we going out tonight? Unless you've already got a date? Think you could squeeze me in?"

Dawn began to laugh — her own sweet, low chuckle that sounded to Pete like love itself.

She stood up, and he followed suit, and they embraced and kissed so intensely they were unaware of the mob of police, of the rounding up of Monty, or the arrival of Mr. Chrystal.

"I guess Chrystal Falls isn't so bad, after all," said Dawn huskily, stroking his face.

"It *is* bad," said Pete ruefully, "but there are some pretty good people here. You, for example. And me."

"You," agreed Dawn, smiling at him, "are the best example of all."

Chapter Fourteen.

The night was late.

Above the soaring glass roof of the new Chrystal Mall was a black, star-studded sky. Along the wide expanse of the mall, soft romantic lights made gentle circles of warmth. Tiny spotlights focused on the immense crystal chandelier and sent rainbows darting over the pale walls.

The band was playing a slow number. The dancers were pressed close together. Heads and cheeks touched, and hands were clasped.

The fountain itself danced. Water burst into the air and cascaded down over glaciers of glass to fall into the blue-tiled pool below.

On the pool's wide rim sat Karen, leaning against Mitch. They had danced every single dance for two hours. Karen had slid her shoes off at some point and not found them again. "I love you, Mitch," she whispered.

"Do you love me enough to let me skip the next dance?" he wanted to know. "I think I need a week of rest and relaxation."

Karen snuggled against him. How wonderful he looked in his tuxedo! How she loved him!

Across the room a camera crew had just finished interviewing Chelsea Chrystal. It was a victory for Chelsea. She knew she had been perfect, and she could hardly wait for the eleven o'clock news. She did not know that the crew had filmed many a beautiful girl in many a beautiful dress, and they were faintly bored. The camera moved slowly across the crowded room to capture the feeling of celebration there for the news program — and it found Karen and Mitch.

No director could have arranged an act so full of young love as that tiny scene the camera found. And the colors of that gown — perfect for television. As the camera zoomed in, Karen and Mitch looked at each other, and very slowly, their eyes sending messages even the finest camera could not catch, their lips moved together.

The crew grinned in spite of themselves. Jaded they were, and they had covered a thousand stories already this year — but they hoped the news director would not cut this particular moment from the story.

Luckily Chelsea did not notice. She was getting congratulations from everyone on handling her first television appearance so brilliantly. George Palmer thought she was destined for stardom. Her father thought she had made him very proud. Her mother thought Lavinia had found the finest dress in all New York City.

· But the opinion Chelsea wanted was Josh's.

They had come together — but had he forgiven her? They were prince and princess together, had danced several dances together — but how did he really feel about her?

When the attention was momentarily off her, Chelsea said to Josh, "I still feel so rotten about Dawn."

"Don't," he said. "It was all of our faults, including Dawn's. Nobody wanted to admit something awful could happen, and Dawn didn't want to admit she just had bad judgment. Let's stop worrying. Monty's gone and everything's fine and — "

He broke off. Chelsea stared at him.

He licked his lips, hardly able to believe she was there with him. The dress was indescribable, not like anyone else's. Pale peach, of the thinnest imaginable fabric, it fell in many unequal layers, like the fountain of Chrystal Mall itself, clinging to her slender frame and trembling with every breath she took. Her smooth hair was a crown of gold.

" — and I love you," finished Josh.

Tears sprang into Chelsea's eyes. She had done her worst — and she was still loved. "Oh,

Josh!", she whispered, and she kissed him fiercely, with gratitude, and then, the old Chrystal strength coming back to her, she kissed him again, possessively, sure of herself.

Mr. and Mrs. Chrystal watched them. For the first time in days they did not have to think of Monty. He had been removed to a private reformatory in the Southwest, where he could be outdoors most of the time, working off the rage that continually possessed him. They were admitting family guilt and paying for the replacement of the gazebo, although Monty denied that he torched it, and there was no proof against him.

It was a closed episode now, and one they would not think about again, until Monty's eventual release forced them into it.

But that was too many years away.

"You are the loveliest girl in this room," said Alexander Chrystal to his wife.

She smiled, delighted at the compliment and knowing it to be ridiculous, because she was wan and frail after weeks in her bedroom. "Our daughter is the loveliest. Don't you think Josh is the perfect boy for her?"

"A tennis bum," said Mr. Chrystal scathingly. "We'll have to put a stop to it."

"Oh, dear," said Elizabeth. "But they're so happy together."

Alexander Chrystal shrugged. "She has a mill to run one day," he said. "I think we've admitted our son will never inherit Chrystal

185

Mills. That means Chels and Amy will. Chels has to marry someone with more ambition than a tennis trophy."

"Nobody is discussing marriage," Elizabeth Chrystal laughed.

Her husband shook his head. "I can see things out there between those two that I don't care for. We'll have to terminate this little relationship."

Nobody noticed Pete and Dawn.

But this was their choice. They had wandered to the end of the mall. It was an enormous complex, with five wings radiating from the core where the fountain splashed. In two wings refreshments were being served, and in another one could find a seat to rest. But Pete and Dawn followed the tiles into the dark of a wing that did not even have its stores rented yet. It was merely a dark passage.

Pete could not keep his hands off Dawn, nor she off him. As they touched each other, they shivered, aching for more. Pete drew Dawn into the entrance of an unfinished shop. In the blackness of its angle, they pressed against each other and kissed.

"Sometimes I can't forgive myself," said Pete, his voice rough, remembering Monty.

"It was my fault," said Dawn. "And poor Chelsea behaved just like me, and it was worse for her. She couldn't face what her own brother was. And I refused to face the real Monty, too."

"I have no use for Chelsea Chrystal."

"Let's not get started on that again," Dawn said, knowing it was a topic she and Pete would never agree on.

Pete said to her, "You are the most beautiful girl here."

She laughed in the dark. "How can you tell? You can't see me."

"I can feel you fine," he breathed, and proved it, and they both laughed.

Back on the dance floor, Josh and Chelsea walked among their friends, saying hello to this group, and accepting congratulations on the television appearance from another. "Next weekend, Daddy is taking us horseback riding at a friend's cabin in the mountains," said Chelsea. "I want you and Dawn to come along. We'll have a wonderful time."

Josh was willing to bet there was no cabin. It would be a magnificent second home, where caretakers lived year round and the stable was full of fine horses. "We'd love to," he said. "I accept for us both."

"Good," said Chelsea. "Now let's dance."

They truly danced like royalty, as though they expected people to stare, and people generally lived up to expectation. Even Karen and Mitch looked up momentarily.

"I've sort of forgiven her," said Karen.

"No, you haven't," Mitch said. "I know you. You're just telling me that, so I'll stop you from crossing the room and tripping her."

"Wonder what her gown cost," said Karen.

Mitch groaned. "Who cares? She doesn't match you."

Karen kissed him lightly. "When we go up to the state park next weekend to try whitewater canoeing, you want to ask Pete and Dawn to come along?"

"Sure. When are we going?"

"Next weekend, I said. Can't you keep track of anything?"

"I can keep track of you," he said, grinning broadly, and this time he was the one to start dancing. They danced in circles around Chelsea, giving themselves in to the music with wild abandon. Chelsea could dance like a princess, but Karen could dance up a storm.

They did not know that the storm was yet to come.

There was momentary peace in Chrystal Falls. Nobody could have foreseen that a simple decision of whether to spend the weekend with Karen or with Chelsea would change the course of Dawn's entire life, and affect all of her friends forever.

The water splashed from the fountain, and the prisms of light glittered, and the opening of the great Chrystal Mall was a success.

It would change in one catastrophic week.

What happens when Dawn forgets what she should remember? Read Chrystal Falls #4, THE MORNING AFTER.